Honestly, Katie John!

by MARY CALHOUN

Illustrated by Paul Frame

SCHOLASTIC BOOK SERVICES

NEW YORK • TORONTO • LONDON • AUCKLAND • SYDNEY

Copyright © 1963 by Mary Calhoun. This edition is published by
Scholastic Book Services, a division of Scholastic Magazines, Inc.,
by arrangement with Harper & Row, Publishers, Incorporated.

3rd printing . . . . December 1969

Printed in the U.S.A.

Contents

Street Fair Fiasco

KATIE JOHN CONSIDERED CHEATING. If she peeked at the down cards under the two sixes in her solitaire game, she'd know which six would be the better one to move. No, it wasn't fair to peek. She put the six of diamonds on a black seven and turned over the card under the six. A black three — nowhere to put it. What if she had moved the six of hearts? There wasn't anything wrong with checking it, now that she'd made her move, Katie reasoned. She looked at the card under it. Another black seven! Now she could never move the red six, for the black seven under it was the only card left to put it on — fiddle! But she must be honest. She mustn't change things now. It wasn't fair to cheat.

Even though she knew she couldn't win, Katie John played out the game on the parlor floor. It was still cool in the dim, high-ceilinged parlor — thick brick walls kept the summer-morning heat out — and light through the slats of the inside shutters wavered on the carpet as tree branches moved outside. The room was like a deepwater cavern, Katie John thought, with hazy pools rippling on its floor. She moved her arm in the yellow-green light, watching the light catch the gold of the hairs on her brown skin. "I'm a golden fish lazing in the bottom of a cavern," she thought, "waving my fins." Dreamily she wove her hands in the green shallows of light. No — she discarded the idea — she wouldn't be a fish popping her mouth open all the time.

There — she couldn't move another card. The game had gone against her, just as she'd known it would. Oh well, better things than winning at solitaire lay ahead today. The Street Fair was waiting! If only Sue would hurry up and come, they could be away to the fair.

Every summer the last week before school started, the Street Fair came to town. Barton's Bluff was the trading center for farming areas around it, so that at fair time people came from downriver, from upriver, from across the Mississippi, and from back country. At Street Fair time all roads led to Barton's Bluff. Main Street was roped off, and carnival rides and tents blossomed in the street between the stores. At the busiest corner a large platform was erected for bands to play on — sometimes the town's brass band, sometimes a western-music guitar band brought in for square dancing. At the other corners were free "acts": this year the Great Rudolpho, walking the high wire each night at 7 and 11 P.M.; Albert and Alberta, trapeze artists; and the Rozzi family and its educated dogs.

2

Restlessly, Katie John started another card game. One more game, then maybe Sue would come, she promised herself, putting out the cards for sidewalk solitaire. She'd learned lots of solitaire games this summer, had spent many a hot afternoon playing them in the quiet parlor. . . . What a nice, lazy summer it had been! Katie stretched happily, thinking back: the week of day camp at the park, where she'd learned to shoot an arrow; the day of the excursion-boat trip on the river, when she and Edwin Jones had explored the engine room of the old stern-wheeler until they'd been chased out; all the fuss and flurry of marrying Cousin Ben off to Miss Julia, with good old Cousin Ben yelling he'd be bing-whizzled if he'd shave off his chin whiskers for the wedding (but he did); swimming with her parents at the old icehouse on the river; the week she and Sue had spent at Sue's uncle's farm.

Abruptly Katie John came out of her stretch. That farm visit hadn't turned out so well at the end. There she'd been, proudly riding the line horse behind the barn, helping to pull the hay up into the haymow. Everything was fine until that pretty yellow butterfly had come along. She'd been so interested in watching it that she hadn't heard the man up in the haymow call "ho" for her to stop. So the horse kept right on going, pulling the line; and the hay fork with the bale of hay kept right on going across the haymow and rammed into the back wall of the barn. It had sort of knocked loose a few boards and broken the hay fork, and all the men had had to quit for the day while the hay fork was fixed. And she'd had to give a month's allowance to help pay for the repairs.

However, there hadn't been any big problems this summer. The Tucker family was well settled in the old house now, and Katie's memories of her former home in California were fading. Now she belonged in this big brick house that her great-grandfather had built, belonged in Barton's Bluff, belonged in the Missouri hills by the Mississippi River. No more quarrels with the renters. Enough money to live on now that Dad's mystery-book writing was going well. And best, all the people she loved around her: Mother; Dad with his jokes; sweet, plump Sue (always clucking like an anxious mother hen whenever Katie set out to do something interesting); Miss Howell, last year's teacher, moving back to her apartment this weekend now that school was about to start — dear Miss Howell.

"Yes," Katie John thought, "life is pretty well squared away. No more worries to nag." After all, what big problems *could* come up now?

She stretched again and yawned. It felt good to be at home with the world. . . . If only Sue would hurry up. She could hardly wait to start for the fair.

Katie John swept up the cards and looked through the shutters to see if Sue was coming up the sidewalk. Instead she saw a whole clutter of people in front. Why, they were having a picnic right out on the stone carriage block. Car parked, doors open, a fat lady in the front seat, a picnic basket and goodies spread out on the stone, grownups and children sitting on the curb eating, a little boy swinging around and around the black-iron hitching post. Must be a farm family come to town for the fair.

The town certainly was filling up, full of hustle and people and excitement. Katie could hear the blare of music from Main Street, a block away, and the rumble of the rides. Today was Tuesday, second day of the fair, Children's Day, when rides were only a dime, best day for families and kids. Main Street must be packed. She couldn't wait. . . .

"I'm going, Mother!" Katie called back to the kitchen, then stopped at the front door. She watched with mounting indignation as the picnicking family tossed away crumpled wax paper and scattered the remains of a bag of potato chips on the grass. Then the little boy who'd been swinging around the hitching post threw up in the gutter.

"Oh, ish!" Katie muttered.

The fat lady eased herself out of the front seat and mopped the boy's face. The rest of the people threw aside bread crusts, brushed off cake crumbs, slammed the car doors, and in a straggling group started down the sidewalk toward the fair.

"Hey!" Katie called after them. "Aren't you going to clean things up?"

Nobody even turned around except the little boy, who stuck out his tongue at Katie John.

"Of all the nerve!" Katie ran out to the front gate. "Hey!"

The family hurried around the corner by Sue's house.

"Well!" Katie John stood with her hands on her hips, looking at the mess around the carriage block. "I've got a good mind to — "

She jumped into action. Potato-chip bags and sandwich wrapping flew through the car window into the front seat. Her nose wrinkled in disgust, she picked up all the potato chips and crusts with finicky fingers and deposited them in the car too.

"There!" She brushed off her hands. " 'Keep the yard tidy,' Mother always says!"

"Katie!" Sue had come out and was waving.

Katie John started to run. But at that moment a small brown figure with a white spot on the end of its tail darted out from a hidden place in the barberry bushes along the iron fence. Confidently, Heavenly Spot ran after his mistress.

"No, Spot. You can't go. You'd get squashed in the crowds."

She motioned toward the yard, but the beagle only lowered his head, all big brown begging eyes.

"Oh Spot, I'm sorry, but you just can't."

She picked up her dog and put him in the house. Then she ran down the block to join Sue.

"What were you doing with that car?" Sue asked.

Katie John told her about the messy family and how she'd cleaned up the trash.

"Oh, honestly, Katie John! You didn't! I don't blame you, though. My mother says Barton's Bluff always looks as if a cyclone had hit it by the time Street Fair Week is over. . . . Do I look all right?" Sue fluffed out her crisp pink skirt.

Katie John looked at her friend in her sleeveless white blouse with the ruffle down the front and the stiff petticoat pouffing out her skirt. Sue's hair curled in little heat tendrils around her face.

"Sure," said Katie. "You always look nice."

Katie had combed her fly-away bangs and put on a skirt in honor of the fair, but that had been the extent of her preparations.

"I wish — " Sue began. "Katie John, would you wear lipstick if your mother would let you?"

Katie stared. "Good night, I just started wearing hair ribbons this year!"

"I would. I tried Janet's lipstick last night."

"Well, I'd feel silly. My mouth would feel silly. It would feel all icky and gummed up." Katie explored the idea. "Maybe I wouldn't even be able to talk like me. My words would come out sticky and smeary and sickly sweet. Why, it'd be like going around with jam on my mouth all the time. Ish!"

"I don't care," Sue said. "I look pretty with lipstick."

The girls walked along thinking their various thoughts about lipstick, then Sue added a defense against Katie's attack on it.

"After all, Katie John, it won't be long before we're teen-agers and wearing lipstick. That's just part of growing up to be a woman."

A *woman?* Katie John tasted the word. And rejected it.

"Huh. We're only eleven years old, and here you've got us practically women already. Hey, Granny," she creaked in a funny old voice, "where's your cane? Why, I've just gotten old enough to enjoy life as a" — she started to say "child" but substituted "kid."

Sue didn't say anything, and that bothered Katie. You couldn't keep proving you were right if people wouldn't argue. She scuffed her toes over each crack in the sidewalk.

At last she said, "Well, all right, how do you do it? Does having a big sister show you how to be a — a teen-ager?"

"Janet? Ugh!" Sue laughed comfortably. "You don't have to learn how to be a woman, Katie John. It just comes along naturally."

Katie didn't think it was at all that easy. In fact, the whole business sounded so hazy and difficult that she just put it right out of her mind.

Now the girls came to Main Street. In the intersection the bronze statue of General Pomfroy on his horse reared up over the hurly-burly and to-and-fro of the carnival. The Civil War hero eternally led the charge, saber in air, indifferent to the village excitement around him. But the two girls had ears, noses, and eyes only for the Street Fair, spread before them with all its delights: whirling rides, flashing lights, hooting calliope music, smells (hot popcorn, hot dogs, hot tar softening under the feet of the crowds — new smells at every step), guns cracking at the shooting gallery, the House of Mirrors, barkers calling ("See the Midget Woman! Tiniest lady in the world! Come in, come in!"), and people. People hurrying, laughing, standing, looking, pushing through a jam, shouting to

friends, waving balloons and pink cotton candy —
holiday people!

"Ahh!" Katie John sucked in her breath, whirled in
delight, and darted into the crowds. "Sue! Come on!"

"Wait." Sue followed more slowly. "Watch out!"

She picked up Katie, who had tripped over a cable
from the merry-go-round, and brushed her off.

"Never mind," Katie said. "Come on!"

And then the girls were part of the Street Fair. They
already knew just what they wanted to do. Yesterday
they had walked up and down Main Street looking to
see what the fair offered, but they'd saved their doing
for today. Both had agreed that the Crazy House
would be the most fun, so they'd save that for a while.
The House of Mirrors must surely be visited too. Katie
wanted to try all the tent shows, but she knew her
money wouldn't hold out. Besides, Sue didn't think
they should go into some of them, such as the Hula
Girl tent. At last they'd picked the Midget Woman
tent to be the one show they'd visit. "Only I'm not
going to look at the snakes," Sue had said, closing her
eyes.

"Me either." Katie John had agreed with one of
Sue's fears for once. However, Katie was determined
to go on the Ferris wheel, even though Sue was afraid
of that as well.

First on the program was the merry-go-round, for
Sue loved it, even though Katie thought it was pretty
tame. They bought their tickets and waited for the
horses to come to a stop. Sue picked a white horse.

"I'm going to ride sidesaddle like an olden-time

.

lady," she said, with a rare flight of imagination.

Katie sat sidesaddle on a green horse, but the ticket taker came around and told them they had to ride the right way or they might fall off. The calliope music began, and the horses started to circle, moving up and down. On the second time around, Katie John saw a large brass ring hanging from the canopy. She'd heard of brass rings, but she'd never been on a merry-go-round that had one.

"Do I get a free ride if I grab it?" she called to the ticket taker.

He nodded, bored.

Next time around, Katie strained out for the ring, but her arm was a good two feet too short.

"That isn't fair!" she said to Sue behind her. "No kid could reach that far."

The merry-go-round people just put it there to tease children, she decided. Well, she'd show them. Next time she passed the ring, she watched to see exactly where it was. Then she pulled her feet up onto the saddle of her horse and crouched, holding to the pole in front of her.

"Katie, don't! Be careful!" Sue cried.

"Nothing's going to happen."

Katie John stood up, holding the pole with her left hand, and snatched at the ring with her right. But the ring was fastened tight to the canopy; it wasn't meant to come loose. As Katie yanked at the ring, her horse moved away from under her. She hung from the ring for a moment. Then it broke loose, and she dropped to the deck of the merry-go-round.

10

The ticket taker came hurrying around. "What happened?"

"I got the brass ring." Katie John held it up.

"Wha—" He stared up at the place where the ring had broken off, then muttered angrily. The horses were slowing to a stop. The man grabbed the ring from her hand and jerked his head at a horse. "Okay! Get on."

"But I don't want another ride," Katie added. "Let my friend have it. See — " she said to Sue, who was looking frightened, "nothing happened."

"Huh!" said Sue, closing her mouth.

After Sue had taken her second ride, the girls walked on down the midway. Next was the Ferris wheel. Sue stayed on the ground and waved to Katie, who called from the air, "I can see the river! There's Priscilla Simmons and Betsy Ann, and some other kids way up the street."

After that they bought popcorn and headed for the Crazy House. Just before it, Katie John paused. A small tent had been set up next to it since the girls had looked yesterday.

GYPSY FORTUNETELLING read the sign. Stars, zodiac symbols, and the palm of a hand were painted on the tent walls. In front on a camp chair sat a heavy woman with golden hoops in her ears. She wore a bright scarf bound across her forehead and knotted in the back. Under it her jet-black hair hung down to her shoulders. She was chewing gum and shuffling a deck of cards.

"A Gypsy!" Katie whispered to Sue. "I've never had my fortune told. Have you?"

Sue shook her head.

"Let's!"

The girls approached the Gypsy fortuneteller. Silently she got up and led the way into the tent, letting the tent flap drop behind them. It was almost dark inside. The woman sat down behind a small table and motioned the girls to two folding chairs.

"Cross my hand with silver," she said rapidly in a gravelly voice.

"How much?" Katie asked.

"A quarter, kid. Make a wish."

Katie John thought and nodded. The fortuneteller began slapping picture cards down on the table, her lips moving, until she came to a joker.

"Twenty-one! You ain't gonna get your wish, kid. Now for what's gonna happen to you."

She put a picture card of a lady in the middle and said that was Katie John. Then she laid out cards in a square around the lady — a star, a tree. "Success, good health," her voice droned.

Katie John looked at the Gypsy's thick fingers, wearing many flashing rings, then up at her brown face. As the woman chewed her gum, her earrings swung with the rhythm of her jaws and her brown mole moved. Could this woman really see into her future, tell what was going to happen to her? How could she know? How could the cards know?

"Here's the jack of hearts, close to your heart."

Katie John squirmed.

"But here's a pitchfork next to him. You gonna drive him away. And here's the queen of hearts, and a sword next to her. Say," said the woman, showing a little interest, "this is the dumbest fortune I ever read. You're supposed to be the queen of hearts, but you ain't."

She popped her gum and droned on. "Letter, lightning next to it, means bad news — something awful's gonna happen. And around to the jack of hearts again, a shovel next to him. What you gonna do, kid, bury him?"

She glanced at Katie John, whose face was dismayed. Hastily the woman added, "No, I guess it means you and he is gonna find buried treasure. Sure, that's it. And that's all."

She slapped her hand on the spread-out cards.

Katie John stared at the pictures, forgetting the woman and Sue. Such a lot of things to happen. Oh dear, would they really? Who was the jack of hearts? The jack on the card was a blond man. She thought of Edwin Jones with his yellow hair. Buried treasure!

"Oh!" she breathed.

"Want your fortune told?" the Gypsy was asking Sue, but Sue shook her head.

Katie John saw a glass ball on another little table at the side. The woman noticed her glance.

"Fifty cents, and I will look into the crystal ball, see lots more, explain your fortune in the cards."

Katie had only fifty cents left, and she hadn't been to the Crazy House yet. But the crystal ball! The very essence of mystery. What strange pictures might the Gypsy see in it? For that matter, how *could* she see pictures in it?

"How does it work?"

Katie picked up the ball to look at it. It was heavy,

and the glass was cloudy. She couldn't see anything in it.

"Hands off the ball, kid! Fingerprints."

The fortuneteller took the ball and rubbed it on her skirt.

"I'd better not," Katie John said regretfully. "I don't have enough money."

"So. Your loss." The woman shrugged.

The girls stepped through the tent flap and blinked at the sunshine and the noise of the fair.

"Do you suppose she really was a Gypsy?" Sue wondered. "Goodness, Katie John, I didn't want my fortune told after I saw yours."

Katie's eyes weren't seeing the street.

"Buried treasure," she murmured. "But where should I dig?" Then she shook off the spell. "Oh, probably she makes it all up. Come on, let's go to the Crazy House."

But the jack of hearts and a *pitchfork?*

After the Crazy House, which was just as much fun as the girls expected, they decided to try another ride. Wandering up the street, they came to the platform where Josh Carney and his western band were playing fast guitar music for the square-dancers. The girls stopped to watch.

"I bet Gladys and Pearl spend all week here," Katie John thought.

Gladys and Pearl were two women who had rented a room at her house last winter. Katie hadn't liked them very much, but she'd learned to get along with them. They loved western music, and their radio had blared with it all the time they were home. Finally they'd had a quarrel, split up, and moved away. The only renter left in the house right now was Mr. Watkins, the night watchman. Mr. Peabody had taken a job upriver. And Mr. Peters the riverman and little Buster wouldn't be back after all this winter because Mr. Peters had married a maid on the towboat this summer, and they were going to live in Davenport, Iowa, when the boats stopped running. Katie was glad nice Mr. Peters had found a wife. That Buster needed a mother to keep track of him. Two of Mr. Peters' friends — rivermen, too — were going to move into the Tuckers' rooming house this fall, though, when the boats couldn't travel because of ice. And of course Miss Howell would be back. She'd said she wanted to give the newlyweds — her sister and Cousin Ben — some time alone, but Katie thought Miss Howell wanted to get away from Cousin Ben's talkityness. Naturally, Miss Howell would be too nice to say so.

Katie John and Sue moved on.

"Oh, that's what I want to try," Katie said, pointing to the caterpillar ride.

The ride consisted simply of stall seats set in a circle on a deck. When the circle got to spinning rapidly, a caterpillar-striped cover rose up over the seats. That was the fun of the ride — though Katie John thought it looked pretty strange to see a caterpillar racing around in a circle as if it had its tail in its mouth. Whoever heard of a racing caterpillar anyway?

"I wonder what it feels like to be spinning around in the dark under the cover?" Katie John said. "Would

I get dizzy? Or would it be a wonderful feeling, like whirling around in a dream?"

"Well, I'm not going to find out," Sue declared. "I might get sick, and I couldn't get out with the cover pinning me in. I don't like to be shut up in things."

As Katie John bought her ticket, Priscilla Simmons approached sedately, stepping neatly over ropes and waiting patiently for huddles of people to part so that she didn't have to push through them. Accompanying her, like a princess' court, were two other of the "nice" girls from Katie's room at school, Carole Jo and Betsy Ann. Priscilla, small, with silky fair hair, looked too delicate to be out in the rough-and-tumble of the Street Fair. Priscilla Simmons always made Katie John feel as if her face might be dirty.

"Are you going on the caterpillar?" Good heavens, her voice had come out so loud, almost yelling, for goodness' sake.

"Oh no," Priscilla said gently. "Most of these rides are too rough for me. I don't like these wild things like you do, Katie John."

Katie John felt shaggy as a bear, hearty as all outdoors. And hateful toward Priscilla. Yet you couldn't say Priscilla was being snippy. It was just that she was so nice, so very, very per-*nicety*-nice.

Howard and Sammy and Pete came rowdying up to Priscilla's little cluster of girls. Katie John had seen the boys only a few times this summer, coming sweaty and dirty from the baseball field, or on other boy business. Now the boys looked bigger, older, almost strangers.

Howard flipped Priscilla's curling ponytail with his

finger and said, "Dare you to go on the caterpillar with me."

Priscilla pursed her lips. "Howard Bunch, you go away! I don't know why you keep following me."

She switched away from him. But Katie John saw her smile a quick little secret smile to Carole Jo. It was no wonder dainty Priscilla didn't like Howard, for he was the biggest, roughest boy in the class. But then why did she smile? And Howard, he didn't seem a bit hurt by her tone of voice. He kept right on joggling around Priscilla and talking to her, and she didn't try to get away, for all her complaining about his following her. Katie shook her head, perplexed.

The caterpillar ride had stopped now, and Katie got into one of the seats. The boys followed, and Howard clambered into the seat beside Katie.

"Okay, Pris, if you won't go, I'll ride with Katie John," he yelled, laughing.

"Oh no you won't!" Katie said.

But the ride had filled up, and now there were no other seats for Howard to move to. Looking around, Katie John suddenly realized that she was the only girl on the ride. There were a few teen-agers and a sprinkling of little kids, but mostly there were boys about her age. Oh dear, it didn't look right for her to be the only girl. How could that have happened? It wasn't *that* wild a ride, was it? Katie John looked toward the girls in the street, half ready to get off again.

Priscilla was watching her while saying something to Betsy Ann. When she saw Katie's glance, she smiled, saying, "Don't let that Howard pester you. . . . Sue, don't Howard and Katie look cute together?"

Cute! Katie John stood up, but the ride started with a jerk, throwing her back into the seat. And they were off! The ride circled, gaining speed, spinning faster.

"I'll hold you down," Howard shouted, grabbing Katie's shoulders.

"Let go!" The words were sucked away from her by the speed.

They whirled past the girls, who were all giggling except Priscilla. Katie had a flashing glimpse of Priscilla's face, and it wasn't even smiling.

Then the boys were yelling, for the caterpillar cover was rising. With a thud, it shut down in a hoop over the circle of seats. Katie John had the sensation of being pulled along against her will in total blackness. The ride wouldn't wait — she was going away from herself too fast to think what it felt like. After a moment of dizziness, she began to feel she'd caught up with the ride, and her eyes adjusted to the darkness. She could see a few heads in the tunnel of seats as it curved away. Katie gasped, trying to get her breath, the force of the spinning pressing her stomach against her ribs and her ribs against the outer edge of the seat. Howard, on the inside, was thrown upon her, and she shoved at him.

"You're squashing me!"

Now the galloping caterpillar was slowing its rush. Katie's stomach came back into place as the ride came to a stop. Now the cover would lift — but it didn't. The canvas stayed clamped down.

The teen-age boys began whooping and whistling. "Hey, lift the lid!"

"Get a can opener!"

"Let's cut our way out! Where's a knife?"

Over the hubbub the ride attendant shouted, "Wait, folks! Just one moment. The switch is jammed. We'll have you out in a minute."

Katie John heard some woman outside say, "Can they breathe under there?"

Oh, for pity sakes. She hadn't thought of not being able to breathe. She sucked in hot, dusty air.

"Oh dear!"

"Don't be silly," Howard said. "You've been breathing all along, haven't you?"

The girls outside were screaming, and Katie heard Sue running around the ride, calling, "Katie! Where are you?"

"Here!" She poked the canvas.

"Katie! Katie! Are you all right? Oh dear, can you breathe? I just knew something awful would happen!"

Immediately Katie John felt better. "Oh Sue, don't be such a mother hen. This is fun. It's not everybody that gets shut up in a caterpillar."

Actually, it was more like being shut under a very low hoop of a covered wagon, and it wasn't really much fun. The canvas had a very distinct and bitter smell. The air was close and dusty. And it was *hot* under there. Katie wiped the sweat from her neck. Why didn't they hurry up and lift the cover?

Now the boys on the ride were doing what boys always do when they're kept waiting with nothing to do — wrestle and roughhouse. The canvas billowed and shook as they crawled over the seats, punching and scuffling and yelling.

"Who is it?"

"Hey, I gotcha!"

"Look out!"

Outside a crowd must be gathering. Katie John heard lots more voices.

"What happened?"

"The cover's stuck."

"Hey, look at that caterpillar shake! It's got the heaves!"

Howard couldn't exactly wrestle with Katie John, so he did the next best thing. He tickled her. Katie couldn't help squealing and laughing.

"Howard! Stop it! Stop it, I said!"

It's no fun to be tickled. Katie John squirmed, shrieked, and laughed in spite of herself and punched at Howard. Sammy and Pete came crawling over the seats.

"Sock him, Katie! Come on! Fight! Fight!"

Howard kept on tickling, and Katie squeaked and gasped, "Sammy, help! Howard, quit it!" She twisted, trying to get Howard's fingers, trying to stomp on his feet.

She heard a man outside ask, "What's going on in there?" and another man shouted happily, "They've got some girl in there. Boy, listen to her squeal!"

Oh! Oh, the embarrassment! Katie John ducked her head and bit Howard on the hand.

"Ow!"

At that moment the canvas cover rose.

"Hooray!" the crowd shouted.

Katie John jumped off the ride and ran to Sue,

who'd gone back to the cluster of girls. She took big breaths of the good outside air and twisted her skirt around into place. Howard and the boys came laughing after her.

Sue smoothed at Katie's hair. "Oh, Katie John, are you all right?"

The girls were all talking at once, and Howard was shouting, "Whee, was that fun!"

Priscilla's sweet voice cut through the chatter. "Honestly, Katie John! How could you laugh and have so much fun under there with all those awful boys? But then, you like boys, don't you?"

Katie stared at her. "What do you mean, I like boys?"

"Well, nothing, Katie. I just mean you're good with boys. You like boys, and they like you. You've started dating, haven't you? I saw you with Edwin Jones on the excursion boat. You better watch out, Howard." She smiled at him.

Katie John listened with mounting horror. Her chest felt squeezed.

"Dating! Are you crazy? I *hate* boys!"

She'd never particularly thought so before. Boys were just other kids. But now, suddenly, she decided it was true. Noisy, stomping, heavy-footed boys. Of course it was true. And besides, Priscilla Simmons couldn't stand there in front of everybody and say, "Katie John likes boys."

"I hate boys!" Katie repeated. "They're terrible, awful, nasty things!"

"She sure does. Look where she bit me." Howard showed his hand, laughing.

Katie John didn't hear him, for she'd turned away angrily after she'd spoken and come face to face with Edwin Jones. Edwin, her good friend of the summer's adventures. How long had he been here?

He looked at her silently. Edwin never wasted words.

"Edwin, I —" What could she say in front of all these kids?

In a low voice he muttered to her, "Forget about biking out to Wildcat Glen tomorrow."

He turned and trotted away into the crowds.

Oh! Worse than boys, Katie hated that Priscilla Simmons!

Treasure at Wildcat Glen

THE REST OF STREET FAIR WEEK was ruined. Katie John couldn't stop fretting about Edwin Jones. It was not only the loss of the bicycle trip to Wildcat Glen that she minded. She hated to be at odds with Edwin. They'd had such good times this summer, exploring along the Mississippi banks and swinging on the grapevines by the river, biking out to a little pioneer cemetery that Katie had found, reading together a wonderful book about the discovery and digging up of the ancient city of Troy. Edwin wanted to be an archaeologist or an explorer when he grew up — he couldn't decide which. Maybe both.

Katie John had missed something in her friendship with Sue, and she'd found it in Edwin. He wasn't afraid to do exciting things, though he didn't plunge ahead the way Katie did, and he had interesting ideas when you got him to talking. He was fun to be with, and now everything was ruined. All because that Priscilla Simmons had made her scream around about how she hated boys.

As for the Street Fair, the music and noise from Main Street kept Katie awake at night so that she could worry more about Edwin. She did enjoy watching the Great Rudolpho on the high wire, especially the heart-plunging moment when he missed a step and then it turned out to be all pretend. However, by the end of the week Street Fair was mostly a hot confusion of noise and litter.

The only really bright spot in the week came on Friday, when Katie John helped Miss Howell, her fifth-grade teacher, move back into her apartment at the Tuckers' house. She'd missed her former teacher while Miss Howell spent the summer out at her farm on the River Road. Of course Katie and Sue had ridden their bicycles out a few times to see Miss Howell and her quiet sister, Miss Julia, who'd married Katie's Cousin Ben. But it hadn't been the same. Last winter Katie would bring the wood up for Miss Howell's fireplace, and then they'd sit by the fire and talk about books and faraway places. Mother had laughed and said Miss Howell was Katie's second mother. This winter Katie John expected things to be even better; last year she couldn't be chummy with Miss Howell at school because she hadn't wanted to seem teacher's pet.

When Katie John had been carrying in suitcases, of course little old Miss Crackenberry next door had to hurry out to weed her garden so she could watch the proceedings. Katie John had given up trying to believe Miss Crackenberry was a witch, but the old lady certainly was tart as a lemon. As Katie started into the house with a second load of Miss Howell's bundles, Miss Crackenberry had called her over to warn her, "That dog of yours has been chasing my little Prince again."

Katie John looked Miss Crackenberry straight in the eye (she could, for now that she'd grown she was as tall as the tiny woman) and said, "Miss Crackenberry, I can't help it if Heavenly Spot chases Prince when Prince snaps at him first."

She moved back as Prince sniffed nervously at her legs. You never knew when he might bite. Prince was a bad-tempered little dog who was the unfortunate result of mixing breeds. He looked like a Pekinese in the head and tail, but he had a short-haired fox terrier body.

"I see you haven't learned any manners this summer," said Miss Crackenberry. "No wonder, chasing around with a wild boy." To Miss Crackenberry, all boys were wild.

Katie John's face burned. Edwin again!

The little neighbor lady continued her attack. "I see somebody's moving in. Are your folks going to fill the house up with rough renters again this winter? Emily Clark would turn over in her grave if she knew what you folks have done with her house."

"She wouldn't mind," Katie started to argue. But she gave it up. No good ever came of arguing with Miss Crackenberry. Anyway, it wasn't any of her business why the Tuckers had chosen to rent out rooms in the old house. Really, it was because they needed the money to live on while Katie's father was writing books. Now that he'd sold one book, there was more money, and they were going to rent rooms only to Miss Howell, Mr. Watkins, and the two rivermen who were coming later. Katie and her mother wouldn't have to work so hard anymore taking care of so many rooms and renters. But there was no use trying to explain to the crook-nosed old lady.

"Good-bye, Miss Crackenberry," Katie said as politely as she could force herself. "I have to go help."

By Sunday morning Katie John was in a nervous snit about Edwin. Her hands were so cold she could hardly hold her hymnbook as she marched into church with the other choirgirls. Edwin probably would be here for Sunday school, and then what would she say to him? How would he act? At least Priscilla Simmons wouldn't be here to say things; she went to another church. But Howard Bunch was in their Sunday-school class. Anyway, she wouldn't have to sit in the choir loft with that awful Howard. This fall the choir directress had decided to have only girls in the choir.

While the minister was reading the first lesson, Katie looked to see if Edwin was in church. By leaning forward just a little she could see him sitting almost behind a pillar. He was looking at her! Hastily she leaned back and fixed her eyes on the minister. Oh dear, Edwin's face had looked cold. After the opening service, all the children went to their classes. Edwin didn't sit near her, nor did he look at her. Katie John didn't look at him either. Howard tried to start something, but the teacher stopped that by putting him to work filling in a map of Palestine on the blackboard.

Katie John didn't learn a bit about the journeys of the apostles in Palestine. For all she knew that Sunday, they could have been walking around China. She was too busy not looking at Edwin. And thinking. Edwin was still mad. Obviously he wasn't going to do a thing about fixing matters up. Here school was about to start Tuesday, and if she didn't do something quick, maybe they'd go the whole school year being not-friends. Besides, she told herself, she'd so wanted to go to Wildcat Glen, and only Edwin knew the way. The place had such a wonderful, shivery name.

After class, Edwin volunteered to put the folding chairs away in the basement. So he was going to keep busy in order not even to walk out near her. Katie John walked to the door slowly and stood trying to decide whether to go out or what. She saw Edwin head down the basement stairs with an armload of chairs. There wouldn't be anyone else in the basement — Katie John made up her mind and ducked down the steps.

She found him back by the furnace stacking chairs. "Edwin?"

He looked up, startled. "What do *you* want?"

"Well, I just wanted to say —" Goodness, what did she want to say?

Rapidly, "Well, when I said that at the fair it was just that Priscilla — I mean — well — well, Edwin, I didn't mean I hated *you*."

"You said you hated boys."

"But — I meant *boys*. You're not a *boy*, you're just you."

"I am too a boy. You said boys were terrible, awful, nasty things. And I'm a boy, so that must be what you think of me."

Edwin spoke as coolly as if he'd been explaining to her how a frog's legs worked. Why did he have to be so logical? And all this you-me stuff — it made her nervous.

"Look, Edwin, do you want to go out to Wildcat Glen or don't you?"

"Sure, I do. But I can go alone."

Katie John turned to leave. Her voice came out small. "It's just that it's more fun with somebody."

There was a silence as she walked toward the stairs. Then behind her, "Okay, meet you at the cemetery gate at two o'clock."

She couldn't look back. "Okay." She nodded and hurried up the steps.

Katie John ran all the way home. Now everything would be all right. While her parents were at the eleven o'clock church service she set the table for Sunday dinner. She wanted to get the meal over with as soon as possible.

After dinner Katie set out on her bicycle, which she had named Explorer. Of course Heavenly Spot went along too. He always accompanied her on her jaunts to the woods, running alongside with his long ears flopping, his eyes on his mistress, his brown tail waving its white tip. That is, he ran alongside the wheels in town; in the country he'd be off over the fields snuffing after rabbits. Heavenly Spot loved trailing nearly as much as he loved Katie John.

Katie John smiled down at Spot, thinking of the hymn she'd sung this morning, one of her favorites, in which one gave thanks for things like lambs and gallant horses and stars. And "For dogs with friendly faces," she sang out, "we thank you, Lord, for these."

"You want to trail a wildcat, Spot?" she added. "Maybe you can today."

Heavenly Spot looked agreeable.

Actually, no one had seen a wildcat around Barton's Bluff for years. But once a wildcat had been seen in Wildcat Glen, and that's how the place got its name. The story went that two men had been out hunting possums with their dogs. The men heard a strange cry down in a rocky hollow, and they saw what looked like a wildcat. The dogs had taken off after the creature, yelping and scrambling up the creek bed back into the hills. The wildcat was never seen again. And neither was one of the dogs. It was a mystery what had become of the dog, and the name "Wildcat Glen" had stuck to the place. Ever since, children had visited that particular creek, which otherwise looked no different from the others running down to the Mississippi, shivering in hopes they'd see the wildcat — at a good distance.

"I wouldn't really let you chase the wildcat," Katie told her dog. "You might disappear, too."

Heavenly Spot waved his tail and looked agreeable.

Katie John pedaled up the side street that led past the cemetery. Yes, there was Edwin waiting on his bike at the gate. Edwin lived there with his father, who was the caretaker. Edwin got his way of talking with few words from his father, who was a very quiet man. Sometimes Katie wondered if living in the cemetery made them that way. She liked the little green hills and hollows of the cemetery, the tree-shaded quiet, and the interesting gravestones, so she could understand why Edwin didn't mind living in a grave-yard. Priscilla Simmons and some of the girls always acted so silly about it though, as if Edwin might have a ghost in his pocket, for heaven's sake.

Katie John didn't want to get involved in any more of that embarrassing you-me business, so she started right in talking as she rode up to Edwin.

"Hi! Spot's going to catch the wildcat."

Edwin knelt to play with Spot, rolling him over to rub the sensitive spot on the dog's stomach that made Spot's hind legs scratch the air.

"I'll bet. You'd trail that big cat, and then it'd turn around and make a meal of you in one bite. Wouldn't it, fella?"

Heavenly Spot looked agreeable.

Edwin could talk to dogs better than he could talk to people. It was too bad he couldn't have a dog of his own, but some folks wouldn't like a dog to live in the cemetery. It might run over the graves.

"What do you think of having a man teacher this year?" Katie said as they rode on.

"Be okay, I guess."

"I hear he's queer. I mean, he calls everybody by their last names — 'Tucker, go to the blackboard. Jones, pass out papers' — like that. I wonder if he's awfully strict."

"I wonder if he knows anything about archaeology. Say, that reminds me."

Edwin told Katie about a magazine article he'd been reading on undersea archaeology. It was something very new, made possible by the advances in diving equipment.

"Just think," Edwin exclaimed. "They might find sunken Roman galleys. Find out all kinds of stuff about ancient trade routes on the seas."

Katie John thought about Edwin and his archaeology and asked curiously, "How come you aren't crazy about exploring space like the other boys are?"

"They want to see where we're going. I want to see where we've been, that's all."

"It's just as much of a mystery, isn't it?"

Edwin corrected her. "Not *just* as much. Quite a bit is known about the past. But there's lots more to find out."

Presently the road dipped low near the river, and they were at Wildcat Glen. The creek of the glen ran under a small bridge in the road and on down to the river, but Katie and Edwin wanted to explore up the glen back into the hills. They dragged their bikes into some bushes and walked into the hollow. Along the creek bed ran a grassy ravine with rocky banks on each side. It was the dry end of summer, so the creek ran in a small trickle.

Katie John was hot and thirsty from the ride. The water looked good, and she knelt to scoop up some in her hands to drink.

"Hey, don't!" Edwin grabbed her back. "It might be impure. Probably runs through a pasture somewhere."

"The water runs over rocks."

"But it's not full and swift enough to clean itself now."

Katie John bowed to male authority. She'd pay attention to Edwin when she wouldn't listen to grown-ups or even Sue. Mostly because Edwin was usually right. She'd found out that when Edwin held back on some adventure, it wasn't because he was afraid but because holding back made sense.

Heavenly Spot had been sniffing around the glen. Now he approached the stream and slupped up water.

Katie John hauled him back by the tail. "Spot! Don't!"

Heavenly Spot looked agreeable. But when she let go, he went right back to drinking the water.

"Edwin?" Katie appealed.

He shrugged. "I never knew of a dog dying from drinking impure water."

Katie had heard that the creek came from a spring out of the rocks up in the hills. She'd never drunk spring water cold right out of the ground, and she suggested they try to find the spring.

This time it was Edwin who looked agreeable, and they set off up the glen along the creek, with Heavenly Spot dashing around them trying to decide which of the interesting animal smells to follow. It felt good to walk in the cool, damp glen after the hot ride. Along the way Katie and Edwin looked for geodes, a kind of rock peculiar to that area. Geodes looked like plain old round rocks on the outside, but broken open, the insides were sparkling crystals, like huge diamonds. Once Edwin pointed out some walnut trees up on the banks.

"Walnuts later this fall."

"Yes, we can bring sacks."

Then Katie noticed that Heavenly Spot wasn't with them. He must be off following one of the smells. She didn't really expect to meet a wildcat in the glen; still, she wanted Spot to stick close to them, just in case.

"Here, Spot."

No answering bark.

"Here, Spot. Here, Spot. Here, Spot Spot-ty!"

Katie John listened. The only sound was a small gurgle of the creek. No sounds of dogs barking or automobiles, not even wind in the trees. How still it was in the glen. So remote. . . .

"Oh, Edwin, do you suppose the wildcat got him?"

Edwin smiled. "No."

"But he always comes —"

"Leave him alone, Katie. He'll come when he's ready."

"No. I've got to find him right now," she insisted. "Come on."

Katie John, followed by Edwin, headed back down the glen calling and calling. Soon they heard a burst of excited barking far off to one side.

"There he is! Oh, that dog!"

Katie John scrambled up the steep bank, sending a shower of little rocks down on Edwin, coming after her. They climbed up out of the glen and ran through the trees, guided by Spot's "I've-got-something-cornered!" yaps.

The trees ended, and they came out into an open field on a hill overlooking the Mississippi. In the field was a weathered gray farmhouse, and at one corner of its foundation was Heavenly Spot digging frantically at a hole.

"After a field mouse," his mistress said in disgust. "I thought maybe he had the wildcat cornered. Spot, come away!"

"You know, this place looks deserted," Edwin said.

It certainly did. The glass was broken out of the windows, and the roof of the back porch had fallen in. A rusted plow lay by a tumbledown shack of a barn, and trash was scattered in the yard. Weeds had grown up around the house, choking out flower bushes. A rosebush had gone wild, and a tangle of its thorny branches reached into the house through a window.

"It looks like the brambles all grown up around Sleeping Beauty's castle," Katie exclaimed. "Or a witch's brambly house. . . . Look." She ran into the house — the front door was gone — and put her face up to the window where the rose-tangle grew in. She made a horrible grin. "Don't I look like a witch looking out through the thorns?"

"Huh. Some witch. With pigtails?"

Katie John and Edwin left Spot to his yapping and digging while they explored the place.

There was no doubt about it. The house was dead. In the front room where Katie had put her face to the window, streaked, no-color wallpaper hung in torn strips from the walls. Some floorboards were broken through, and there were shotgun shells scattered about, as if hunters had stopped there. Only one of the front-room windows still had glass in it. And yet the house wasn't completely bare. There were still some ancient furnishings about. A large old heating stove stood in the front room, its stovepipe gone, and along one wall sagged a long, old-fashioned couch, upholstered in some kind of prickly hair. Springs stuck up out of holes, and the upholstery was chewed bare in spots.

"That certainly doesn't look comfortable." Katie John plumped herself down on the sofa, and a whoosh of dust rose from it.

"Look out," Edwin warned. "You may be sitting on a nest of mice."

She got up hastily, and they went into the next room. Across the middle of the house ran a large dining room. On one side of it a staircase began and turned up to the second floor. On another wall was a built-in china cabinet with most of the glass broken out of its doors.

"Why, there are still some dishes in it," Katie said. "Not good ones — these look like old junk. But why would people leave anything at all when they move away?"

"There are still some things in the kitchen, too," Edwin called from the room behind the dining room.

Katie John ran to look. Sure enough, in the big kitchen was an old iron cookstove, a table, a sink with a hand pump in it, a high-backed rocking chair. While Edwin tried the pump — only air came out — Katie lifted one of the round iron lids on the stove. And dropped it back with a clatter.

"Something moved in there!" she gasped.

"Let's see." Edwin lifted the lid again. "Hey, it's a nest of baby mice."

"Oh!" Katie peered into the dark insides of the stove. Crawling around amidst litter were tiny mice with big ears that showed pink and clean on the insides. "Oh, aren't they cunning!"

"Don't pick them up," Edwin advised. "The mother

might not take care of them when she comes back if she smelled human on them."

Katie John had no such intention. She was not afraid of mice, but her bravery did not extend to handling them. She watched them, however, as Edwin hunted along the kitchen shelves to see what he could find.

"Here's a book," he reported. "A *Farmer's Almanac*, 1925."

As Katie looked up she noticed something on the wall by the stove. "Here's a calendar, still."

She studied it. At the top was an old-fashioned picture of a boy hugging a woolly dog. Below the picture the pages were torn off down to July, 1932.

"Edwin, you know what this means!" Katie exclaimed. "Whoever lived here left in July, 1932. Nobody's lived here since."

"They could have left before July," Edwin said logically. "Hunters or somebody could have torn off pages since."

"But the family was here some time in 1932," Katie insisted, "or they wouldn't have hung up the calendar."

"Yes, and look here at these clippings."

Articles and pictures cut from newspapers and magazines were tacked all over the wall above the sink. Edwin ran his finger over them, hunting for dates on the papers. He and Katie found several: May 18, 1926, November 29, 1931. The latest one seemed to be February 4, 1932. Of course not all the clippings had dates on them.

"It certainly looks as though they were here until 1932," Katie said. "But why did they leave some of their things behind? Of course most of it is junk, but you'd think they'd take that rocker and the almanac."

She remembered when she and her parents had moved from California. They'd packed up every single thing, and then scrubbed walls and floors. When they'd left, the rooms had been completely bare and already echoing with loneliness. She cried then, though now she was glad she'd come to Barton's Bluff.

"You know, Katie John," Edwin said slowly, "maybe the family left even more stuff than is here now. It looks as if this place has been deserted for more than thirty years. A lot of kids and people could have carted off an awful lot of things in that time."

"You mean — they could have just picked up and left suddenly — left everything?" Katie felt strangely frightened by the idea. "Edwin, do you suppose they all were eaten by the wildcat?"

Edwin laughed one of his rare out-loud laughs, breaking up the lonely feeling. "Oh Katie, you and your nutty ideas! That wildcat would have popped! Come on, let's see what's in the barn."

There wasn't much of interest in the barn, which held a few broken-down stalls and a rustle of mice where the hay had been stored. A frayed rope hung from a rafter, and in a corner was a small clutter of rusted chain, a broken lantern, and some bits of what might have been some kind of farm machinery — things Katie didn't recognize. She and Edwin decided that the upstairs of the house, yet unexplored, might hold better possibilities.

Heavenly Spot had given up on the mouse and followed them upstairs. There was even less of interest in the bedrooms than in the barn, however. They were quite bare. And then Katie John found the one treasure in the deserted house.

Of course she'd opened every door, and at last in one bedroom she came upon a low door the height of a four-year-old. She tugged it open and found a small storage attic under the sloping roof of the house. She crawled into it. The shut-up air was hot and stuffy, and it was dark in there — but then she spied something.

"Edwin, a box!"

The carton was heavy as she shoved it out into the bedroom for more light.

"Oh, just magazines. Still, I wonder what kind of magazines they read?"

She lifted them out. There were old copies of women's magazines, *Collier's,* and *National Geographic.* The cover pictures looked more and more old-fashioned as she dug deeper into the box.

"That's all," she said, taking out the last magazine.

And there at the bottom was the treasure: a small narrow box, and inside, a fan. The ivory handle was carved out in a lacy filigree, and a ring of ivory hung from the handle. Carefully Katie John spread open the fan, and the silk, though yellowed with age, didn't crack. In faded blues and pinks and browns, delicate butterflies were painted on the silk. They seemed to flutter and dance as Katie waved the fan in front of her face.

"How lovely!" she breathed.

And how strange to find something so delicately beautiful in a tumbledown old farmhouse.

"Do you suppose I could have it?"

"If you want." Edwin shrugged. "Everybody else has taken what they wanted from here. Though that fan sure doesn't go with your pigtails."

"Huh! I guess I can take my hair *out* of pigtails if I like."

Katie John started to put the magazines back in the carton, and then she noticed something else in the bottom, a small square of hard paper. She turned it over and saw that it was a picture of a young woman, showing just her head and shoulders. It was a very old photograph in fading brown. At first glance the picture looked something like the drawings of girls Katie had found in an old book in a bookcase in her house one rainy day. Then Dad had told her the drawings were by an artist named Gibson, made in the early 1900's, and the type of girl had become known as the Gibson Girl. This girl wore the same kind of high-necked blouse, and her hair swirled in a pouf around her head, held back by a wide band. And yet she wasn't like the Gibson Girls exactly. Forgetting Edwin, Katie John studied the photograph. This girl didn't have the wide, sweet face of the Gibson Girls; her face was small and came to a pointed chin. Her nose wasn't straight and serious either; it was more of a snub. And what were those spots under her eyes? Freckles! This must be an untouched-up photo — a proof maybe.

"Edwin, look." Katie showed it to him, laughing without knowing why. "I like her."

Edwin stared at the photograph, then smiled. "You know why? She sort of looks like you."

Katie John looked at the picture again. "Oh, I don't know about that. I just think she looks friendly."

But freckles? And the fan? Had this woman owned the fan? They didn't seem to go together. Had this girl flirted with a fan and hidden her freckles behind it?

Slowly Katie John put the picture back in the bottom of the box and stacked the magazines on top of it. The fan and the picture surely were from the early 1900's — long before the 1930's, the date on the calendar downstairs. Had the family lived in this house for generations, the way Katie's ancestors had in Great-aunt Emily's house, the old Clark place?

Edwin had gone back downstairs, and Katie followed him, carrying the fan box. She found Edwin examining the front-door frame. He pointed to the top of the frame, and she saw faint scratches in the wood, outlined with years of dirt. Twisting her head, she read, "Calkins, 1910."

"I thought I'd find it here," Edwin said triumphantly. "In the old days a house builder often carved his name and the date of building somewhere on the house."

Katie asked if it was the name of the carpenter or the family who owned the house, but Edwin wasn't sure. Katie looked down at the fan box in her hands, then back at the scratchings.

"We've just got to find out more about who lived here. I know! The newspaper clippings. Maybe they're wedding stories, birth announcements — sort of a family history in clippings."

She and Edwin ran back to the kitchen, where

Heavenly Spot was yapping happily at the stoveful of mice. However, the clippings didn't seem to have anything personal about a family. There were pictures of birds and of boys on a raft, articles on baby care and California. But nothing that seemed to tell who'd lived here.

"Let's ask about this place when we get home," Katie John said. "Surely somebody in Barton's Bluff will know the story of this place."

"Katie, no!" Edwin's usually cool face blazed with the excitement of an idea. "I've got it! Let's study this place the way archaeologists would. We'll find out who this family was all on our own, like hunting down a mystery!"

Archaeologists learned how ancient peoples lived by digging up the things the people left behind, he reminded Katie. Sometimes they'd find old walls, and they'd dig trenches deeper and deeper, hunting for things such as old pottery and tools, things that would tell what the people were like, how they'd lived.

"And we don't even have to dig," Edwin said. "All sorts of clues are left here — the date on the door, the calendar, the clippings, the fan, the stuff in the barn. Everything's a clue. Bit by bit, we'll piece things together."

"And then we'll know!" Katie John was caught up in the idea. "And when we're done, we can check with some old-timers in town to see if we're right!"

"Well, all right —" Edwin agreed with that part — "though the archaeologists don't have anyone to ask if they're right."

The afternoon had a very late feeling by now, and

Katie and Edwin decided they'd better go home. Edwin wanted to come back the first thing the next day, Labor Day, but Katie John had to go on a picnic with her folks. Then Edwin remembered, reluctantly, that he had to stay home tomorrow anyway, to help greet and settle an aunt who was coming to cook for him and his father this winter. And school started the following day. At last Katie John and Edwin agreed to ride out here next Saturday, as soon as they'd finished their chores, and bring their lunches so they could spend the day.

Even though it was late in the day as they left the house, Edwin insisted on following the grassy ruts that led away from it. The path — you couldn't call it a road any more — curved away through the woods, and there were even young saplings growing up in it. Edwin said they could try to figure the age of these little trees, and so get some idea of how long it had been since the road had been used. Before long the path came out on the Wildcat Glen road, not far beyond where they'd left their bikes.

Katie John placed the fan box in her bicycle saddlebag. Pedaling back to town, she thought of the treasure she was carrying home. Edwin must be right. Everyone had carried away what he wanted or needed from the deserted house. And then Katie wondered, why had the freckle-faced girl no longer wanted or needed her fan? Why had she left it behind?

Boy-Haters of America, Unite!

THE FIRST DAY OF SCHOOL! A sunny, fresh September morning, the world all new again, and the summer-deserted school grounds swarmed with children and excitement. In the summer when Katie John had passed the school, the playgrounds had always looked so deserted, swings hanging down empty, teeter-totter boards gone, stored away. Even when a few children were on the playground, idling on the merry-go-round in the hot sun, the place had looked lonely, all the school windows blank eyes with the shades pulled down.

Now the windows sparkled, freshly washed, and the playgrounds had come to life again with a shout. Surely all these crowds of children would never fit into the brick school! Katie John stood with Sue, happy and eager. What would the new year bring? How would she like a man teacher? And what fun it was to be in the sixth grade, the biggest kids in school now!

Ignoring all the little children darting around, Katie looked for people in her room. Round faces she hadn't seen since last spring had slimmed down, bodies were taller. There was Rhoda Phillips, fatter even than last year. Rhoda liked to hang around Katie. Pete Hallstrom was as tall now as Howard Bunch, who'd been the tallest boy in their room, but Pete looked just as pole-skinny as ever, not big and chunky like Howard. They were wrestling in the dust, and their mothers would have fits if they saw those new jeans smeared up already. Edwin must not be here yet. All the girls were decked out in new dresses, and Priscilla Simmons had the most darling dress of all, naturally. Her mother bought Priscilla's dresses in St. Louis or had them made. Katie didn't mind. She had on a pretty new dress too, and Mother had cut off her pigtails in a soft, short haircut in honor of school's starting.

Actually, cutting off her braids had been Katie's idea. Yesterday morning she'd awakened with Edwin's remark about her pigtails rankling in her mind. "That fan sure doesn't go with your pigtails," he'd said. She'd fretted about it as she helped her mother get ready for their Labor Day picnic. She guessed she could look just as pretty with a fan as the next girl. Mother was good at cutting hair; she was always shaping her own. Finally Katie came right out and asked Mother to cut off the braids. And after the first startled moment, Mother agreed, saying it might be a good idea, now that Katie was getting older.

For once Katie could hardly enjoy the picnic and the swim in the river. She rushed her parents home early, and the grand haircutting event began. Mother spread papers on the kitchen floor and sat Katie on the kitchen stool. At the last moment before beginning, Mother stood before Katie, clicking the scissors in her hand.

"I don't know, honey," she said uncertainly. "It might not turn out right. Your hair is straight as a string."

"No, it will be lovely. Come on," urged Katie John.

So Mother snipped away. And then Katie did feel a pang of sadness as she saw the brown locks falling to the floor. The hair looked so soft. Now a part of her was gone. She hated to lose anything of herself, even hair. She'd felt the same way once when the dentist had had to pull one of her teeth.

"Oh dear," Mother mourned. "I was afraid of that."

"What? What's the matter?"

Katie John jumped off the stool, spilling pieces of hair, and ran to look in the mirror in her room next to the kitchen. Oh, horrors! It used to be that just her bangs were spiky. Now all of her hair hung in spiky wisps. The shape of the haircut was all right, but her hair didn't hang together. She looked awful.

Katie John began to cry.

Mother came into her bedroom. "Honey, honey, don't cry. It'll be all right. I know exactly what to do. You need just a light permanent to give body to your hair."

And sure enough, everything had turned out all right. Mother had dashed downtown and found the one drugstore open on Labor Day, bought a home-permanent kit, and had given Katie her first permanent wave that evening. This morning when Katie combed out her hair, soft shining waves cupped her face, though Mother had left the bangs alone and they were just as spiky as ever.

Katie John touched her hair and wondered what

Edwin would think. Of course he'd better not think she'd cut off her hair just because of what he'd said!

There he came across the playground now. Katie started toward him, but just then Howard shouted to her.

"Hey, Katie John! In case you didn't know, human bites are very dangerous. My hand got infected where you bit it."

He held up his hand, a white club of bandages wound round and round.

"Oh, Howard!" Katie exclaimed. "Let's see."

She waited in anxious silence as Howard solemnly, wincing a little, unwound the bandage into a long strip trailing onto the ground.

"See?" He stuck out his hand. It was perfectly all right. Except for one thing: drawn in ink on his wrist was a skull and crossbones.

"Ha, ha!" Howard shouted. "Where Katie John bites — death!"

Then he fetched up a rumbling belch, perfected by weeks of practice.

Katie John felt an actual pain of revulsion as she looked at Howard's face, red and laughing. She wondered how she could ever have played with such a repulsive creature.

"You know, Howard Bunch, you're — just — plain — disgusting!"

"Yes, he is," put in Priscilla, who was part of the crowd that had gathered as Howard unwound his bandage. "It's no wonder you hate boys, Katie John. I do too!"

"Aw, come on, Katie," Howard said. "You don't really hate boys. Why'd you cut off your pigtails if you didn't want to look pretty?" He ruffled her hair. "Pretty, pretty girly-girl!"

Oh! Katie kicked his leg furiously. Pete and little Sammy jostled around her, pulling at her hair and chanting, "Pretty, pretty girly-girl!" In a red rage Katie kicked out at them too — kicked at every boy within range.

"Get away from me! I said I hated boys, and I meant it! Get away from me!"

The boys hopped away, holding their legs where Katie's pointed shoes had made contact, and the girls crowded around Katie as she wiped her hot face and breathed heavily.

"Good for you, Katie John! Maybe that'll teach those boys!"

"Yes, nasty things! Now maybe they'll leave us girls alone."

"Boys are so awful. I wish I could go to a girls' school." That was Priscilla.

Katie John expanded under approval. "And those boys better not come around me again," she declared loudly enough for the boys to hear, "or I *will* put the poison bite on them!"

Then she saw Edwin walking away. Her stomach jumped. He knew she didn't mean him — didn't he? She broke away from the girls and hurried after him.

"Edwin. When we go to Wildcat Glen —"

He kept right on walking, his back to her.

"Edwin?"

"Hey, Edwin, look out," that terrible, awful Howard shouted. "Katie's gonna put the bite of death on you!"

"I am not!" Katie John faced Howard. "Edwin's not nasty like the rest of you boys."

"Oh, *ho-o-o!*" Howard laughed. "Edwin's a nice boy, huh? Nice enough for a pretty girly-girl to play with. Is Edwin a pretty girly-girl too?"

Sammy and Pete chimed in. "Edwin's a pretty girly-girl!"

Katie expected Edwin to rush at the boys, throwing punches. Instead he whirled at her, his face white. His voice gritted low with fury.

"From now on, stay away from me, you hear!"

Katie John stared at him. Tears burned her eyelids, and she struggled to keep from bursting out crying.

"All right for you, Edwin Jones! You can just keep your old Wildcat Glen! I'll never speak to you again as long as I live!"

The bell rang then, and they all went in. The first day of school was ruined for Katie John. While the class went through the business of meeting Mr. Boyle (who seemed as stiff and clipped as his small, squared-off mustache) and passing out new textbooks, Katie brooded about Edwin. It was just like a selfish boy to blame it on her when it was all Howard's fault. Until Howard came along everything was fine; she was just quietly minding her own business. Actually, Edwin was even more repulsive than Howard, because she'd trusted Edwin to understand. Why should he pay more attention to what Howard said than to what she did? Katie felt uneasily that she wasn't making sense.

And that made her even madder at Edwin. Now he was trying to make *her* feel in the wrong, and she *wouldn't* feel in the wrong. None of this was her fault. If only people would just leave her alone — boys, that is. Yes, Edwin was the most repulsive boy of them all! She hated him!

Katie John caused a mild ruckus when Mr. Boyle assigned seats according to his prepared chart. Sammy was seated behind Katie, and Edwin was to sit cater-corner from her in the next row one seat ahead. Katie gathered up her new books and stood.

"Mr. Boyle, I can't sit here," she said.

"Why not?"

"I won't sit near a boy. I hate boys!"

There. She'd said it in front of a teacher. Now it was official.

Immediately Priscilla and Betsy Ann stood up with their books in their arms.

"Mr. Boyle, may I have my seat changed too?"

"I can't bear to sit by a boy either."

Howard and some of the other boys jumped up or waved their hands in the air.

"Mr. Boyle, Mr. Boyle. I can't stand to sit by a girl. Girls stink too bad."

Mr. Boyle looked down at his seating chart, tapping his fingers on it. His mustache went quirky, but he got a good grip on his upper lip with his teeth.

Then he said in quite a cool voice, "Ladies, gentlemen, I cannot spend the entire morning shifting seats. It is quite impossible to separate *all* of the girls from *all* of the boys. You will please remain in the seats assigned to you."

The rest of the children sat down, but Katie John remained standing. She couldn't sit in front of Sammy, never knowing what that little rat was up to behind her back.

"Miss Tucker."

"But, Mr. Boyle, you don't know Sammy —"

"Sit down."

The words came straight out of the freezer. Katie John sat.

Some school year this was going to be! She could see it already. Every time Sammy did something to her, it would turn out to be all her fault. And what a teacher, after sweet Miss Howell!

At morning recess Katie John walked out with Sue, complaining bitterly, while Sue made anxious little noises and tried to say things weren't nearly as bad as Katie thought. Priscilla Simmons and her little clan of girls came to stand with Katie, while Rhoda and a few others tagged after.

"Katie John, I'm glad you brought it out in the open," Priscilla said. "We all hate boys, and now they know it."

"Yes, Katie." "You were right." The girls chattered and nodded in righteous agreement.

For just a moment Katie John wasn't sure she liked the idea of Priscilla lining up on her side. A few days ago she'd been mad at Priscilla for making her say she hated boys. But now that she thought about it, she decided it was all right. She *had* hated boys all along. She simply hadn't realized it before. The way Edwin had spoken to her!

"Girls, it's war." Katie broke through the chatter.

"We all hate boys, and we'll show them once and for all."

"Yes!"

"What'll we do?"

Katie John thought. "First of all, none of us must ever speak to a boy, or even look at him if we can help it."

"Yes," said the gentle Priscilla, "and every time a boy does something to a girl, like pulling her hair or shoving her, *all* of us will rush at him and kick him."

"Agreed?" said Katie John.

All of the girls except Sue said "yes" eagerly.

"There's just one word for boys," Katie John continued. "'Repulsive.' Whenever — if ever — we have to mention a boy, we'll say a 'repulsive.' Like, 'Look out, here comes a repulsive.'"

"We ought to wear badges that say 'We Hate Boys' or 'We Hate Repulsives,'" one of the girls said.

"And we could have club meetings to figure out awful things to do to boys," Rhoda added.

Katie John shook her head. "No, that's paying too much attention to them. We don't want them to think we even know they're alive. The idea is to freeze them out."

"But a club would be fun."

Katie John decided maybe it would be a good idea to organize on this thing, but they'd have meetings only if it was necessary to plan some terrible revenge in case a boy did something really awful. Then, of course, if they were going to be organized they had to have a name.

"The Boy-Haters Club," someone suggested.

"I know — Boy-Haters of America!" Katie said. "And our slogan will be, 'Boy-Haters of America, Unite!'"

She laughed in excitement, glancing at Edwin, who was punching the tetherball, before she remembered she wasn't going to look at a boy.

Then Sue threw a monkey wrench in the machinery. She didn't want to belong.

"But Sue!" Katie John stared at her dependable old friend. "You don't *like* boys, do you? Bob didn't even speak to you today."

"I don't like boys, but I don't hate them either," Sue said stubbornly. "Bob never did anything mean to me."

Sue and Bob had never made a big fuss about being "boy friend and girl friend," but everyone had always accepted it that they would choose each other first for spelling bees, send each other the nicest valentines — things like that.

"But you don't want to be left out," Katie told her.

"No," said Sue miserably. "But I don't hate boys."

Katie John took her off to the side. "Look, Sue, don't you honestly think Howard and Sammy and Pete acted terrible before school?"

Sue agreed.

"Well then, what's lots worse, do you know what Edwin said to me?" She whispered in Sue's ear. "There. If Edwin could say that after being so nice all summer, how do you think Bob would act if he felt like it?"

At last she wore Sue down, and Sue agreed to join the Boy-Haters of America. However, she said she wouldn't ever kick a boy. Katie said she'd kick twice, once for Sue, and they left it at that.

Rhoda wanted to elect Katie John president of the Boy-Haters, but Katie said they were all in this together and there shouldn't be a president. Unofficially, however, Katie and Priscilla became known as Chief Boy-Haters.

In the warm September weeks that passed, the girls waged an effective freeze-out campaign against the repulsives. If a girl had to pass out papers, she stared into the air over a repulsive's head as she handed him his. No girl would correct a repulsive's arithmetic paper. Mr. Boyle gave up the Friday spelling bees for the very first time — naturally all of the girls refused to be on a team with boys, so of course the girls' team won.

Before the first day of school was over, every boy in the sixth grade knew that he was now a repulsive. Howard and some of the boys retaliated by calling the girls "stinkers." But that was such a pitifully weak word beside "repulsive" that it carried no sting.

Before many days passed, a repulsive shoved a stinker, and all the girls, led by Priscilla, closed in on the repulsive, kicking and screaming. Other repulsives came to help, but they were at a bit of a disadvantage because the stinkers used their full powers at kicking, whereas the repulsives had been trained "It's wrong to hit a girl." After the second encounter — with the result that a number of boys limped up and down the classroom aisles — Mr. Boyle ruled that there would be no more fighting on the playground. Any boy or girl seen fighting would do five pages of arithmetic. The boys stopped shoving girls, and the girls congratulated one another that they'd won.

There was no question of boys and girls playing together at recess. The boys played baseball, and the girls skipped rope. Katie John had made up a new chant for skipping rope. As the girls jumped up and down they sang, "I hate boys, and boys hate me. I'd rather be a stinker than act repul-sivel-lyyy!" At times the girls linked arms and walked around the playground, singing Katie's chant in loud, happy voices.

Sue hung back from all this, however, and sometimes Katie saw her glancing at Bob.

At first schoolwork suffered, for the repulsives and the stinkers were too busy hating each other to pay much attention to lessons. Then Betsy Ann suggested that another way to get at those repulsives would be to recite lots better than they did in class and get better grades on papers. Some of the more studious boys rallied to the competition, but the girls usually outshone the boys.

Katie John had an uneasy time of it, however. She couldn't concentrate very well during study periods, never knowing what Sammy might be up to behind her back. Thank goodness she didn't have pigtails any more for him to pester. Still, he could and did sprinkle pencil shavings on her hair, which fell out in a shower when she got out of her seat. And he could and did pin insulting notes on the back of her blouse, with such unoriginal instructions as "Kick me." What was worse, he kept up a constant whisper under his breath, "Katie is a stinker, Katie is a stinker," annoying as the buzz of a mosquito.

One day Katie John reached into her desk and let out a shriek that disrupted class. She'd put her hand into a squirming mess of worms. She didn't know whether to blame Sammy or Howard or Pete. So she settled it by squirting all three the next day with her mother's perfume atomizer that she'd smuggled to school.

Edwin stayed out of the war. If anything, he was more quiet than ever. Sometimes he played a fierce, unshouting game of football with the boys; at other recesses he stayed in the classroom, reading the encyclopedia. A few times his glance accidentally met Katie's, and his eyes were cold blue stones.

Despite her ruling, Katie John found herself looking at him quite a bit during class — how could she help it? The dumb old back of his head was right in her line of view toward the blackboard. She hated the way one piece of his silly chicken-feather hair stood up in a tuft at the back of his head, and it was ugly the way his thin nose poked out from his face in side view. She wondered if he'd gone back to Wildcat Glen. Was he finding out lots about the family who'd lived at the deserted farm? It would have been such a wonderful adventure. And Edwin had to go and spoil it all. Probably he liked exploring there better without her. Unhappiness spread in Katie's chest. It seemed as if every day was a grubbly day, despite the fun of getting even with those repulsives.

Often as Katie John undressed at night she looked

at the fan, which she'd hung over her bed, and wondered about it. She'd shown the fan to Mother when she first brought it home, but she'd asked Mother not to tell her anything about who'd lived at the farm, even if Mother knew — in keeping with the idea that she and Edwin would figure it out for themselves. Now, sometimes, she was tempted to ask Mother or Miss Howell about the family, just to get the mystery off her mind. Miss Howell might very well know, for her home-place farm was out along the River Road in the Wildcat Glen direction. However, for some reason Katie John put off asking.

One evening Miss Howell brought up the subject of the repulsives-stinkers war.

"My dear, you girls are making it very hard for Mr. Boyle to teach."

"I'm sorry, Miss Howell, but I can't help it," Katie John answered. "This is something bigger than all of us."

Matters at school were especially difficult at gym period. The girls refused to be on any teams with the boys, and they ran themselves windless trying to beat the boys' team at relay races. Dodgeball was out of the question because of the kickings that resulted. One day at gym time Mr. Boyle led the class into the school gymnasium.

"We are going to learn square dancing," he announced firmly.

He turned on the record player, and the bouncing music played out over the cries and exclamations of the boys and girls. Mr. Boyle explained that they'd begin with an easy form of square dancing and that the steps went so. The shouting died down as the children watched, fascinated, to see the stern Mr. Boyle bobbing through the steps, his back as straight as ever. Then Mr. Boyle asked Priscilla to help him demonstrate how the steps and allemandes were danced with partners.

"Partners!" The hubbub rose worse than ever as Mr. Boyle and Priscilla neatly faced each other, turned, swung around, and skipped on home. Mr. Boyle turned off the music.

"Now then, each gentleman will choose a lady for his partner."

"Wha-at!"

"Lemme outa here!"

"No sir, I'm not gonna dance with any old (girl) (boy)!"

Mr. Boyle spoke over the protests and shrieks: "I have anticipated this difficulty. As you do not care to exercise a choice, you will be assigned partners."

Amidst groans, the teacher read out the assignments. Betsy Ann and Howard were partners, Priscilla was to dance with Sammy, Sue with Bob, Rhoda Phillips with Edwin, and so on down the list. Katie John hardly knew her partner, a short boy named Charles, who had freckles on his cheeks and a hole in the knee of his jeans.

Mr. Boyle arranged the class in squares of four couples each, and without music the children went through the steps slowly. At first there were a few scuffles of kicking and pinching. But then Mr. Boyle turned on the record player, and everyone was busy concentrating on keeping up with the music.

Katie John could hardly bear to touch Charles' sweaty, repulsive hand, and Charles looked off over her shoulder, his nose wrinkled. He would have done better to watch his feet, for he kept stumbling, and Katie came down hard on his foot whenever it got in the way. When she felt more sure of the steps, she looked around to see what the others were doing. Oh! That traitor Rhoda was chattering away to Edwin, though Edwin was silent, head down, watching his feet. He didn't look as if he were enjoying swinging the large girl around. Good! Katie hoped Rhoda would land on Edwin's foot and smash it! That Sue. Just as Katie expected, Sue and Bob were smiling and talking to each other. However, Priscilla gave Katie John a pained "Oh-Katie-isn't-this-terrible?" look as Sammy swung her around. And Betsy Ann was grimly concentrating on her feet, ignoring Howard, who was laughing as usual. Gracious! Didn't that moron ever stop laughing?

Afterward, in the rest room, all the girls complained loudly about how awful it had been. To have to actually *touch* those repulsive creatures! And how mean Mr. Boyle was to start such a thing! And "do you suppose we'll have to do it again next week?" That two-faced Rhoda complained along with the others. Katie John didn't speak to her. Instead, she turned to Sue, who was combing her hair.

"Sue, I saw you talking to Bob. You were enjoying it!" Katie accused.

Sue laughed. "But Katie, don't you think square dancing is fun?"

"Certainly not!"

The following week there was less energy in the repulsives-stinkers war. Other things came up to take attention. The music teacher organized a sextet to prepare a song for the PTA meeting. Katie and Sue were chosen, and a girl named Helen whom Katie didn't know well. The girls practiced in the music room during recesses. In class everyone was busy with a project for the South American studies. On a table at the back of the room they were making a large papier-mâché contour map of South America, with stick figures and appropriate miniature products to place on various countries.

When Friday came, Mr. Boyle led the class to the gymnasium again. The girls were all atwitter. Would they have the same partners? How could they bear dancing with that three-footed Howard (Sammy, Charles, Raymond, Pete) again! Mr. Boyle stood by the record player. He said that they would do the same square-dance steps of the previous week.

"Gentlemen, you may choose your partners," he added.

At first the boys scowled, muttered, and stayed where they were. Then Howard said to Pete in a show-off clear voice, "Might as well pick somebody who won't stomp all over your feet."

Grinning, he walked over to Priscilla. Priscilla pulled in the corners of her mouth and threw Carole Jo a martyred glance, but she didn't object. The other boys followed Howard's lead. Bob picked Sue, and Pete chose Betsy Ann. Katie watched Edwin from the corner of her eye. He waited, then walked over to Rhoda. Hmph! Katie John was afraid that terrible Sammy would pick her. Then, as most of the boys and girls paired off, she suddenly worried that nobody was going to pick her. With the last reluctant boys, Charles walked up to her, not looking at her. Katie John felt as grubbly as she had in a long time. All rumpled and discontented and unhappy. Why had Mr. Boyle ever dreamed up square dancing!

Mr. Boyle turned on the music, and the bobbing and handing around proceeded. Katie was disgusted to see quite a few girls laughing with the boys. And of all amazing things, even Priscilla looked as if she were enjoying the dancing. She was actually smiling at Howard!

After it was all over, Katie John went up to Priscilla, who was whispering to Betsy Ann in the rest room.

"Priscilla, are you a Boy-Hater or aren't you?" Katie John asked point-blank.

Betsy Ann snickered, and Priscilla's dimples showed in a little smile.

"Of course I hate boys," Priscilla said lightly.

"Then why were you laughing and talking with Howard?"

"Was I? Oh, Howard's not so bad, Katie. At least, he gets a firm grip on your hand so you don't go sliding all over the place. I like a boy to know what he's doing."

Katie John looked at her. "You like a boy," she exclaimed. "How can you say such a thing, Priscilla Simmons — you, a Boy-Hater of America!"

Priscilla shrugged. "Boys are awful, but Katie, don't you think that this Boy-Haters Club is getting sort of childish?"

"Yes," Betsy Ann added. "We can't keep fighting boys forever. We've got other things to do."

Katie John didn't know what to say. At last she said, "Okay," and turned away. When she glanced back, Priscilla and Betsy Ann were whispering again. The other girls in the rest room were talking about square dancing and the boys.

The war between the repulsives and the stinkers was over — for everyone but Katie John.

Who Am I?

KATIE JOHN sat at the round dining-room table doing her homework. Her parents sat in the parlor, reading, with the folding doors open between the two rooms. Katie John was with her parents, yet apart.

That's the way she'd felt all week at school: there, yet apart from the other children. She still hated boys, though her energy for doing anything about it had drained away. As for the girls, something was happening to them. Katie John couldn't put her finger on it, but somehow they seemed to be changing. She hadn't even felt very close to Sue.

Although it was Friday night, Katie concentrated on her social-studies notebook. She'd been rather neglecting her studies since school started, and she didn't want Miss Howell to think she'd become a poor student. It didn't matter what Mr. Boyle thought. Katie didn't feel at all close to him either.

In the parlor Mother said, "Listen to this, Hugh," and read something aloud to Dad. And then Dad wanted to see the book, and Mother said she'd never get it back and they laughed together, and Katie John ignored them. Ears out of focus, eyes out of focus, she stared unseeingly at the dining-room sideboard. Why did she feel so different from the other girls? Was she different? Was she different because she was an only child living in a big old house?

"I love the house my great-grandfather built," Katie John said softly, testing the sound of the words.

She wandered out the dining-room door to the hallway and looked at the spindles of the staircase rising to the second floor. On the wall by the dining-room door was a round white-glass shade covering a gas fixture left over from the days when the house had been lit by gaslight. A cupid and flowers were painted on the shade. Katie John was fond of the cupid, and she ran her fingers over the smooth roundness of the glass.

Then she walked up the stairs and sat in the half-dark on a step near the top. It was a good place to sit, with lots of house spread around her. Below was the first floor, with the basement under that. She could see the front hall with light pooling out on the floor from the parlor. A white chandelier hung over the newel post at the bottom of the stairs, and a small marble-topped table bore a copper bowl of marigolds. On the level of her head was the second floor, and above that another whole third floor of rooms. Behind her, a wing reached back down the steep hill on which the ninety-year-old brick house was built. So much room to spread out in, so many parts of the house to go to.

"When you come into this house, you're in a different place from anywhere in the world," Katie thought. No, that wasn't saying it just right. "This house is a little country all its own" — that wasn't exactly it either. Anyway, it was different from living in the little California house they'd moved from. There you knew every corner and were as soon outdoors as in. Here. . . .

Katie John rested her elbows on her knees and her chin in her hands. She listened to the silence of the house. No sound from Miss Howell's apartment on the second floor; no furnace hum, for it was only the first week in October, and the furnace wasn't turned on yet; no street sounds, for the thick walls kept them out. A rustle of Dad's newspaper in the parlor. . . . Now that Katie's ears were sharpened for listening, she felt as much as heard a steady beat, a faucet dripping in a bathroom. Below her a snuffle, a faint scrabble of toenails on wood and a sigh: Heavenly Spot turning over in his sleep in the back hall. Separate little sounds. And under them, a sound that she could almost hear: the house's own sound of quiet. "The house is breathing," she thought. She liked that.

"I'm different from other girls because I live in an old house that I love." Still, maybe that didn't make her different. Probably the other girls had special feelings about their houses, too.

"Nevertheless, I'm different," Katie John thought, relishing the idea. "Living in an old house, a person becomes dreamy, thinks long thoughts." She saw herself tall and slender and lovely — a princess, drifting through a stone castle with tapestry on the walls, floating out to a moonlit balcony where someone sang below. . . . Katie John giggled. "That's not me."

"All right then, if I'm so different, what sort of person am I? Who am I? Well, I'm *me*, Katie John." She laughed at herself. "You're me, you're not some lovely pale princess."

"What will I be? A nurse, an animal doctor? No, besides that, *who* will I be, what sort of woman?"

She'd startled herself. "Me, a *woman?*"

She tried to imagine ahead, but she couldn't. She said to herself firmly, "I'm me, Katie John, who I am right now. *But who am I?*"

Too much thinking. Katie John got up and walked down the dark back stairs to her little room off the kitchen. Now what did she want here?

She looked around and saw hanging over her bed the ivory fan from the deserted farmhouse. She lifted it off its nail and held it in her hands, running her fingers over the lacy carving of the handle. She spread the fan in front of her face and watched herself in the mirror, her eyes looking back at her over the silken butterflies. All you could see were the eyes. You couldn't tell if the person holding the fan was smiling or not.

Had the woman in the farmhouse picture hidden her freckles behind the dancing butterflies? "Oh, silly, it's a *fan*. You're supposed to fan yourself with it when you're hot." Katie John waved it back and forth. It did stir the air. But you could use a folded newspaper to do that, if that's all you wanted. All this dainty silk and ivory simply to stir the air? Maybe you'd use it when you were hot on dainty, ladylike occasions, such as after dancing — huh, there was nothing dainty about square dancing. Had the girl danced, gone to parties, fluttered her silken fan?

"I want to know!" Katie John said aloud. Edwin or no Edwin, tomorrow she was going back to Wildcat Glen. She'd find out about the girl and the fan by herself.

The next morning, though, being Saturday, Mother wanted Katie's help with the housework. Mother and Dad were going to wash windows, so she told Katie to wash the breakfast dishes and clean up her room and dust and vacuum the dining room and the parlor.

"Why do your orders always have 'ands'?" Katie John flashed angrily.

"Here, here!" Mother said in surprise.

Katie John tried to explain that she had to get out to Wildcat Glen before Edwin should happen along.

Mother only replied, "Did you ever count the windows in this house?"

Mother wouldn't understand on purpose! More and more these days, Mother didn't even try to understand. About anything! Not anything at all!

Katie flung herself at picking up things in her room. She rattled through the dishes and whisked the dustcloth over the parlor furniture, not bothering to pick up vases or dust chair rungs. By the time she'd zoomed the vacuum cleaner across the floors, it was ten thirty. Naturally. The morning half gone.

At last she was on her bicycle, pedaling across town with Spot running alongside, and her spirits lightened. Maybe it would be a good day after all. It was lovely early October weather, clear blue sky, leaves turning color, sun just warm enough. When Katie passed the cemetery gate she looked around quickly for Edwin, but there was no sign of him. She hoped his father had enough work for him to keep him busy all day. Though, for that matter, there was no reason to suppose that Edwin had ever gone back to Wildcat Glen, or that he'd be going on this particular day. After all, it had been a month since they'd found the farmhouse.

When Katie John reached the creek, she hid her bike in the bushes and ran into the glen, kicking up a few colored leaves that had already fallen. She noticed that the nuts were thick on the walnut trees. She'd have to come back for them later when they fell. That dumb Edwin. Why had she ever thought it would be fun to go picking walnuts with him?

The glen was as quiet as before, except for Spot's snortings as he hunted smell trails. Katie scrambled up a bank and through the trees. Yes, there was the old gray farmhouse still, just as it had been there since — when was it? — 1910.

Now to study all the details, begin reconstructing the life there. First, the surroundings of the house. The house itself sat near the edge of a bluff, with the view open to the river. Sitting on the front porch, a person could have watched the old steamboats go by or see across to the Illinois shore. Katie wondered if a grandma had sat on the porch in the kitchen rocker, knitting and watching the river. Behind the house stretched a field bounded on three sides by trees. Had the family grown corn in the field, or was it used as pasture? Now the field was all grown over with berry bushes and brambles.

What kind of flowers had the ladies of the house liked and planted? Katie John walked around the house. There were the thorny rose vines gone wild at one side, where she'd put her face up to the window. She didn't know much about plants, but she was sure that the spreading almost tree near the back door was a lilac bush. It looked a good deal the same as the lilac bushes at her house looked now that autumn was here. And what was this little thing? Why, it even had a flower on it still. A little wild rosebush! Katie knew that for sure, for she had one of her own. Great-aunt Emily had planted it, Mother said, and Mother had given it to Katie to be her own to tend. Katie loved the healthy pink flowers with their petals laid open honestly, not all curled together in a tight, formal shape the way most roses were.

"How very old are you, bush?" she said to the wild rose, laying one gentle finger on a petal. "Did someone love you?"

Had the freckled girl planted the wild rose so long ago?

Before Katie did anything else, she wanted to see the picture again. She ran into the house and up the stairs, sending up flat echoes. Pulling the carton out of the storage space, she dumped out the magazines. Ah, the picture. Katie John held the girl in her fingers.

"Who are you?" she said.

The girl-woman didn't smile. She was properly serious for this occasion of having her photograph taken. But there were points of light in her eyes, like a sparkle. And that nose and those freckles could never look serious, Katie thought. Without smiling, the girl looked happy. And pretty. "Much prettier than me," Katie decided. "How could Edwin think she looked like me?"

"Will you quit thinking about him!" she commanded herself aloud in the bare room.

It wasn't loyal of Edwin to turn on her the way he had. He wasn't a true friend, and she ought to quit thinking about him forever. Now her feelings were all rumpled up. But they smoothed down as she turned back to the picture and began figuring. If this house was built in 1910, and this girl looked like the pictures of girls in the early 1900's, then maybe this house was built for her. Maybe she'd come here as a bride! Immediately Katie John knew she was going to proceed on this theory The girl had become the lady of this house, and she'd learn about the girl from studying the house.

Perhaps that wasn't the scientific way. Did archaeologists have a theory about ancient civilizations when they started digging? And then did they watch to see if the pots and things they found fitted their theory about the people who'd lived there? She wasn't sure.

"But that's the way I'm going to do it!"

Now what sort of person was the girl? She'd had cheeks like speckled eggs and a merry look despite her serious lips. How did a girl who looked so honest and everyday fit with a fan that looked like moonlight, music, romance? How had she become a woman who'd used the fan? For that matter, maybe the fan didn't even belong to her. Yet the picture and the fan were together. Katie John was sure they belonged to each other.

Well, she could start with the magazines. What did the girl read? There were old copies of *Ladies' Home*

Journal. On the cover of one was a drawing of a man and a lady dancing. "Romance and Social Number" the cover read. The date was February 1, 1911. Katie turned the pages, thinking of the girl reading the love stories. She riffled through another old *Journal* — a picture of people having tea on the bank of a castle moat in England, advice on child care, hats. Katie laughed at a hat called "conservative." It was larger than the head and swooped out in the back, bird fashion. Had the girl — Katie wished she knew her name — studied the hat styles and how to make a blouse for a dollar?

Katie John decided to give the girl a name, at least until she found out what her name really was. She knew that wasn't at all scientific, but it was too vague to keep calling her "the girl, the woman, the lady." A nice, old-fashioned name — Netta. Now where had she gotten a name like that? She looked at the photograph doubtfully. Netta? Somehow that had to be the girl's name.

Maybe her name was on address stickers on the magazines! Katie hunted through all the magazines, but none of the covers had stickers on them. Oh well, perhaps magazines weren't mailed with stickers back in those days.

Katie John riffled through the rest of the magazines, old issues of *National Geographic, Collier's, Boy's Life. Boy's Life?* Those were more recent, in the 1920's.

Aha! Then boys had lived here. A discovery! Netta had had at least one son!

Katie John reviewed what she'd found. A lady who'd owned a fan lived here, and there'd been at least one boy. Surely a husband too? Had a grandma lived with the family, or a grandpa? Were there daughters? The magazines didn't seem to be able to tell her anything more. She put them back in the box, but she kept the picture of the girl, placing it carefully in her pocket. Then she walked around the upstairs. There were three bedrooms plus a little cubbyhole of a room behind the staircase. Enough room for a fairly good-sized family. But there was nothing in any of the rooms to tell her who'd lived in them. The ceilings were low, the closets cramped spaces under the sloping roof of the house, nothing in the closets.

Katie went downstairs. In the front room there was nothing but the broken-down hair couch and the big stove. Goodness, that stove must have provided the only heat the house had. There were no fireplaces and no registers or radiators from a furnace. Those bedrooms upstairs must have been cold in the winter. She ran back up the steps to check and found the chimney that the stovepipe connected to. It ran between two of the bedrooms, and in each there was a kind of vent in the chimney that could be opened. Well, good, there must have been a little heat upstairs. Just the same — Katie shivered, remembering last winter's below-zero temperatures.

Back downstairs, the dining room had nothing to offer but the built-in china cabinet with the broken glass panes. Katie dragged the rocker in from the kitchen to stand on it to look at the top shelf. Nothing. Oh, why hadn't the family left something forgotten and interesting on the top shelf?

Still, she wasn't discouraged. The kitchen held the

most possibilities, and she'd been saving it for last. A woman spends most of her time in the kitchen, she reasoned, so there she should find the most clues about Netta.

Katie dragged the rocker back to the kitchen with what seemed a dreadful scraping in the silence of the deserted house. She looked inside the iron cookstove, but was disappointed. The mouse family was gone. Maybe the baby mice had grown up in the past month and moved out to the fields, or maybe she'd scared them into moving when she'd looked in before. Surely the mice wouldn't want to move to the fields with winter coming on, though, so maybe they'd gone under the house.

Katie John studied the kitchen, trying to imagine the freckled girl working in it: heavy old black cookstove (it would have heated the kitchen too), battered counter and the sink with the pump in it for water, shelves too high for easy reaching, the scarred wooden table on one wall, rocker in the corner by a window. Of course the floor boards weren't broken then, and the kitchen wasn't so dirty and worn out, yet a feeling of depression came over Katie John. What a dreary place for that merry-looking girl to come stepping lightly. This was a kitchen for a heavy-footed, middle-aged farm wife, whereas Netta, with the wide band over her hair, looked more as if she were setting out for bicycling. Katie was remembering the old magazine pictures of girls in bicycling bloomers. What a dilemma! A snub-nosed girl with speckled cheeks, a silk fan, and a farm wife's kitchen. How did they all connect?

Katie began by checking along all the shelves and in the cupboards under the sink, and found absolutely nothing new. The *Farmer's Almanac* was still on the shelf where Edwin had found it. She sat in the rocker to look at the almanac, reading weather forecasts and planting advice on crops and old-fashioned jokes. Netta's husband must have used this book. Katie John leaned back, rocking with a steady creak. Netta had sat here, looking out the window to the river, perhaps as she did her mending or rocked her baby son.

Sometimes people wrote notes to themselves on calendars. Katie jumped up to look at the 1932 calendar hanging by the stove. No — if anything had been written on the dates, the writing had long since faded away. Well then, there was nothing left but the clippings.

There was no window over the sink; Netta must have put up the clippings to have something to look at as she washed dishes. They covered an area about three feet wide and two feet deep, a hodgepodge of pictures and articles, now yellowed and water-spotted — Netta's picture window. Katie John's heart beat faster as she climbed onto the counter and began reading the top row. There were faded newspaper articles on business opportunities in California and the wonderful California weather, and right below them a picture of a caravan of shaggy camels in Mongolia. It might have been cut out of the *National Geographic* magazine. Katie gave up trying to read the clippings in any orderly fashion and looked them all over. There was a page of pictures identifying various kinds of owls, an article on the proper antidotes to use for different kinds of poisons, a picture of the Himalaya Mountains and one of a castle on the Rhine River in Germany, an article of advice on what to do when the baby has colic — the gist of the article seemed to be to keep the baby's knees warm.

In the middle of the "window" was a magazine drawing of two boys on a raft floating on a river. "I'd like to go rafting on the river someday," Katie thought before her eyes moved on. There were other articles and pictures, but Katie was most interested in a home-made valentine and some children's drawings she'd discovered. Family things!

The valentine was a heart cut out of red paper, not too expertly pasted on frilly white paper, and pasted in the middle of the heart was a tiny picture of a cupid. No writing on it. With careful fingers, Katie loosened the valentine from the wall. On the back was printed in straggling capitals, "I LOVE YOU, MAMA. PATTY."

Netta had had a daughter! And Netta was the kind of mother who'd put up her little girl's first valentine and look at it forever and never take it down.

Now for the drawings. One was a crayon drawing so ordinary that only a mother would have it, for it showed the usual thing a child draws when he's first starting out: a square house with a pointed roof, a big yellow sun with lines for rays, and a tree covered with red dots for apples. The drawing was very faded and smeared by now, yet Katie could make out printing in one corner. It looked like "Wingter" — no, "Winston." Netta's son! The other drawing was on a sheet of lined notebook paper, and the work was quite good.

It showed an eagle in flight, with nice detail and shadings in ink. In dashing script a name was signed in the corner: "Hal Calkins."

Calkins! The same name that was scratched on the doorframe. Katie's mind flashed, putting things together. The Calkins family had lived here, and no doubt Mr. Calkins had built this house for his bride Netta. A young farmer who could build, a young bride with freckles and a fan, then at least three children.

Well, she'd learned quite a bit about Netta this morning! For a minute Katie felt proud of her explorings and deducings. And yet — and yet — she still hadn't found what she was looking for. She wasn't even sure she knew what she'd been looking for, what questions, except that — somehow she still didn't see how the freckled girl and the fan and the farmhouse kitchen could all be a part of the same person.

"Oh, why do you make such a bother?" Katie said to herself. "You wanted to find out about the family like an archaeologist studying, and you did. What difference does the girl make to you?"

Nevertheless, the troubled, unanswered feeling remained.

She hooked the valentine back onto its wall tack and walked out the back door toward the barn. Maybe she'd find some clue in the barn, though she doubted it. She felt as if she were getting "cold," as in the game where you try to find a hidden object by the directions, "You're getting warmer — no, colder," as you walk away from the object.

Katie John stopped. A sound had come from beyond the barn. She wasn't sure what kind of sound except that it was one you didn't hear in deserted fields. Maybe it was Heavenly Spot. For that matter, where had her dog been all this time? She ran forward as softly as she could.

Behind the barn and off to one side toward the woods was a gully, and more rustling sounds came from there. Katie suddenly remembered. The wildcat? She swiveled on the balls of her feet, half tempted to run away, then tiptoed toward the gully until she could look down into it — a spot where rain water had gradually worn the hill away.

And there was Edwin Jones. He was pulling apart the brush and matted grass in the gully. On a cleared spot of the ground by him were laid out an old black purse, stiff with rain and years, a broken pink doll, and other odds and ends, such as a dented coffeepot and some toy wagon wheels. Heavenly Spot lay on the ground by Edwin's collection, watching him.

Katie understood. Here in this gully the Calkins family had thrown away its trash. Edwin had found the place, under the years of brambles and mouse nests, and he was excavating it the way an archaeologist would. For a moment Katie watched him work, carefully, gently pulling apart weeds and scraping at something in the bank so as not to disturb the way anything else buried might lie.

Edwin looked up at her. She hadn't made a sound; even the dog hadn't noticed her. Yet Edwin had felt her presence somehow. Of course. He must have known she was around somewhere, with Spot being here. How long had he known and not even tried to find her? Or had he silently watched her through a glassless window frame of the house?

"What do you want?" Edwin's voice was abrupt, unfriendly. It seemed to say, "I'm busy, go away."

Katie John had a clear memory of her voice that first day of school, saying, "You can just keep your old Wildcat Glen. I'll never speak to you again as long as I live!" So she couldn't answer him. She felt a miserable twisting inside of her. There was Edwin, finding clues about the Calkins family (what could the old purse tell?), and she could have been so much help to him, digging, carrying finds up to the house to keep them out of further weather. It could have been so much fun together. If only they could go back to last summer and start all over again.

When Katie didn't answer, Edwin shrugged and bent his head back to his work.

So he didn't want to make up, be friends. He was just as mean and disloyal as ever. Well, she wasn't going to stick around here with that *boy* acting as if she were a nuisance.

"Here, Spot," Katie called in a strangled voice.

She turned and ran, Spot following, to the other side of the field, toward the place she'd left her bike. When she was safe down the bank into the creek bed of the glen, the tears came. Katie John sobbed, stumbling over the rocks. What a child she used to be, calling bad days "grubbly" days. This wasn't grubbly; it was just plain misery.

Katie's No Lady

O N MONDAY MORNING there wasn't one single good thing about the world. A dark October rain was falling, bringing down the wet leaves in a giving-up sort of way. Katie John felt like the leaves. She'd reached a dead end at learning any more about Netta, there was something wrong with the girls at school, and the thought of Edwin was too painful to touch. The future was as gray as the sky, as dull and unpromising as a bowlful of yesterday's oatmeal — not one good or bright thing to look forward to.

And to top it all, she was late. Unwilling even to get up on such a dreary Monday, she'd lain in bed long after Mother had called her. Now Sue would have gone on, and she'd have to run all the way to school. Over Mother's protests that Katie should eat a hot breakfast, Katie John gulped down a glass of orange juice and a glass of milk and ran out the front door, pulling on her coat. As usual, Mother didn't understand.

Prince was sitting on Miss Crackenberry's front porch, gloomily regarding the wet world. As it often was, his lip was caught up on a tooth in a sneer.

"Grouchy old dog with a rumpled lip," Katie thought, hurrying on. Old rumpled lipskin. Like Rumpelstiltskin. Say! Rumpledlipskin! That was a good name for Prince — Rumpledlipskin. Or Prince Rumpledlipskin. Slightly cheered by the stimulation of a good idea, Katie John ran on to school with a fresh spurt to tell Sue about the name.

However, when she found Sue in the rest room combing her hair with some other girls, Sue was too interested in the conversation to listen to good ideas.

"Sue, you know Prince —" Katie burst in.

"Wait." Sue motioned to her to be quiet.

Priscilla was talking about a seventh-grade girl who lived next door to her.

"Sandy says all the seventh-grade girls are getting them. What happens is, the girls count straps when you're dressing for gym. And if you don't have two straps, you're nowhere."

"What —?"

"Brassieres," Sue whispered. "Shh."

Brassieres! Katie's mouth forgot to close.

"But what if you don't —?" Carole Jo hinted delicately.

"They get size twenty-eight double A," Priscilla said. "That's the smallest, I guess. Anyway, Sandy says all the seventh-grade mothers are buying them for their girls."

Betsy Ann sighed in anticipation. "I can hardly wait until I'm in seventh grade."

Katie John scowled at the girls. Were they *crazy?* Why, if anything, her own chest went *in*.

"Come on, Sue," she said sourly. "If you keep combing your hair forever every day, it'll fall out before you're twenty."

As she and Sue went out she heard Priscilla's sweet little giggle. Betsy Ann and Carole Jo joined in, and Katie was sure they were laughing at her.

Through the week the dreary rain continued, and Katie John's dreary feeling deepened with it as she watched the girls at school. She'd never really paid much attention to them before this year, for she'd been busy with her own doings and Sue and Edwin. Before, Priscilla and her gang had seemed rather dull, never joining in games at recess, always standing on the sidewalk talking about who-knows-what. Now Priscilla and Betsy Ann and Carole Jo were becoming leaders among the girls, with their important talk of clothes and picture albums of popular singers and movie stars. They knew and sang the latest songs, and after school they were learning to dance. It seemed that the girls watched a late-afternoon dance program on television and practiced the steps, dancing together. Even Sue was infected.

"Do you ever turn on that program?" Katie John demanded.

"Well, sometimes," Sue admitted. "Would you like to come in someday and —"

"No!"

After school Thursday, matters came to some kind of a head. There'd been a Campfire Girls' meeting at Betsy Ann's house, and it was Katie and Sue's turn to stay on to help straighten up. Priscilla lingered too, helping Betsy Ann pick up napkins and clean up after the refreshments. Katie and Sue put away scissors and picked up scraps left over from the stuffed animals they were making for children in the hospital. Betsy Ann's mother was off in the back of the house somewhere fixing supper, and the girls had the living room to themselves. When they were done they started to get their coats, but Betsy Ann stopped them.

"Listen," she said, starting to giggle, "let's call up some boys."

"Oh sugar, that's so silly," Priscilla said, taking her coat off again. Priscilla had picked up a cute way of calling everybody "sugar."

"Come on," Betsy Ann urged. "We don't have to say who we are. We can disguise our voices."

She tried to get Sue to call up Bob, but Sue good-naturedly refused.

"I haven't got anything to say to him that I can't say at school. I've known Bob ever since I was five years old, and he'd think I was silly if I started calling him up now."

Katie John was relieved to find that Sue was still her own sensible self.

Meanwhile the other girls decided they'd call up Howard Bunch.

"You do the talking," Priscilla insisted, looking up the number in the phone book.

Katie John watched, half fascinated, half disgusted, as Betsy Ann put a pencil between her teeth.

"Hello," she mouthed around the pencil. "Is this Howard Bunch? Does Elm Street run past your house?"

"Oh boy," Katie John muttered to Sue. "Can't she do better than that old joke?"

"Then go out and stop it!" Betsy shrieked into the telephone. Priscilla put her head up by Betsy's, and they both laughed like maniacs into the receiver.

How could Priscilla change so fast? Just a few weeks ago she had been a Chief Boy-Hater. Even yet at school she talked about the boys being "repulsive clods," but she was paying attention to them all the time, Katie suddenly realized. All this business of clothes and counting straps and dancing and now calling up boys — what it added up to was boy-chasing!

"I've got to go home. You coming, Sue?"

Katie John threw on her coat, hardly waiting for her friend. Outside on the sidewalk she exploded.

"Boy-chasing!"

"Oh well, Katie John, they're just having fun."

"Fun — ha! Popular songs, dancing, calling up boys — you call that fun? Haven't they got anything more important to do?"

Sue murmured soothingly about it being a little thing, but Katie John surged on.

"That's just it. It's *little!* Everything they do is little, silly, giggly. Don't you see, Sue, this boy-chasing— it's such a *little* way of life!"

In her own quiet way Sue was enjoying the feminine business of clothes and dance programs and knowing Bob liked her. So she huffed her feathers a bit.

"Well, all right, Katie John, you know so much — what else is there? I mean, when you get right down to it, you want to grow up and marry a boy someday, don't you?"

Katie John was taken aback. "I never thought about it."

At least, she'd never thought about marrying a *boy*. She'd always vaguely supposed she'd marry a *hero,* which was quite a different matter. She developed the idea: and after they were married a while the hero would come to look something like her father.

"If you aren't going to have dates when you're a teen-ager, what are you going to do?" Sue persisted like a nagfly.

Katie John thought of studying and school plays and good books. Actually, she didn't have many ideas about being a teen-ager. She'd been too busy living life from day to day. Her plans for the future had been more in the realm of "when I grow up." When she was younger and could wrap her legs around her head, she'd planned to be a circus acrobat. Now, since she'd had to remove so many ticks from Heavenly Spot's ears after his trailing expeditions, she'd been seriously considering being an animal doctor. But what to do when she was a teen-ager? Good night, she had enough trouble just being eleven years old.

"I don't know what I'm going to do. All I know is, there's more to life than boys — I hope!" Sloppy, belching, clomping, *disloyal* creatures. Katie John had never felt so depressed in all her life.

In fact, she felt so disturbed that she tried to talk with Mother about it that night as she helped with dishes. Talking about it took the form of telling Mother all about how silly the girls at school were acting these days. Katie John didn't know what she wanted her mother to say, but Mother was of no help. She said in her usual practical way that it was too soon to worry about boys, but that Katie shouldn't condemn the other girls just because she didn't want to act like them.

"But, Mother!"

Mrs. Tucker smiled at her angry daughter. "Honey, that's just their approach to womanhood, growing up."

"Well, I think it's a silly, nutty approach! And if I have to act like that, I'm not going to grow up!"

Katie John threw down the dishtowel, slammed into her room, and fell down on the bed, crying. Why couldn't Mother understand about anything any more? Had she acted silly like the other girls when she was eleven? Mother probably couldn't even remember. Katie John wailed, letting the tears flow unchecked. She noted with miserable satisfaction that her pillow was getting soaked. But when she was done she didn't feel soft and relieved, the way she usually did after a good cry. Something had hardened inside of her.

She knew just what she was going to do. She was going to act exactly the opposite of those girls, with their silly, *little* way of life. If that was being feminine, then she'd be a tomboy to end all tomboys. She'd be different all right, in a big way!

And the first thing she was going to do was take down that silly fan from over her bed. Katie John thrust it in a drawer.

The next morning she plunged into her new role with gusto. Instead of combing her hair in its soft waves, she pushed it back behind her ears. Not stopping for Sue, she hurried to school wearing an old sweater with a hole in it and a rumpled skirt from the floor of her closet. It had stopped raining, and Priscilla, Betsy Ann, and Carole Jo were walking around the playground, arms around each other's waists, singing some popular song. Katie John swaggered after them singing loudly, "Hallelujah, I'm a bum! Hallelujah, bum again!" The girls turned around to stare at her, and she rolled out loud haw-haws.

Then she sat cross-legged on the end of the slide and scratched herself vigorously like an ape. Pretending she was finding bugs on herself, she picked them off and dropped them on the ground. She saw Edwin watching with a disgusted look on his face, so she popped the next pretend-bug into her mouth, smacked her lips, and stuck out her tongue at him. At his shocked look, she laughed a loud jeer. Old Edwin wasn't going to make *her* feel miserable.

Howard came roaring up with Sammy.

"Hey, Katie, you got fleas?" he shouted, ready to join in the fun.

But Katie John did not intend to start associating with boys just because she was a tomboy. She stalked away into the school building. Sitting at her desk, she folded a piece of paper into a pincher that she could open and shut when she put her hand in it. It was an instrument generally known as a "cootie-catcher."

When class started, she quietly pinched her cootie-catcher at the hair of the girl sitting in front of her, though not actually touching the unaware girl. Each "cootie" that Katie caught she pretended to deposit in a little box she'd rummaged out of her desk. Snickers around her told her that Sammy and some of the other boys and girls were watching, though Edwin, cater-corner across the aisle, kept his eyes straight ahead. Once the girl in front of her turned around to see

what the snickers were about, but all she saw was Katie John looking intently at Mr. Boyle, who was talking about Peru.

Now Katie took one pretend-cootie out of the box, smacking the lid back on quickly so the rest wouldn't escape. Pantomiming, she put the cootie through its circus tricks, jumping over her pencil. Then, with exaggerated care, she picked a number of cooties out of the box and pretended to set them in a half-circle on her desk. With her pencil she directed her cootie orchestra.

"Make them sing 'Star-Spangled Banner,'" whispered Sammy, who might be excused for not knowing that the invisible cooties were an orchestra, not a choir.

Absorbed in her cooties, Katie John whispered, "Okay," and hummed under her breath.

"Miss Tucker. What are the principal products of Peru?"

What? Where? Mr. Boyle? Principal products of Peru? It sounded like a chant.

"The principal products of Peru are — cooties!" said Katie John boldly.

The class exploded into laughter, while Mr. Boyle contemplated Katie John in her holey sweater. He waited. Without changing expression, as if nothing had happened, he asked the question again. He wouldn't recognize the incident or engage in personalities. Chilled by Mr. Boyle's calm, Katie John fumbled.

"Well — uh — silver — and —" She named the products she could remember.

At recess it was cootie-catcher time. Howard and

his friends rushed around with their paper pinchers shouting, "Gotcher cooties!" But Katie John took no part. If the boys were going to take up cootie-catching, then she wouldn't. She was different, the lone wolf. When Howard dashed up to her in mistaken delight that the old Katie was back to play with the boys, she told him coolly to go pick cooties off Priscilla, that old sugar-sugar would like it better. All during recess she punched alone at the tetherball, ignoring even Sue, who stood on the sidewalk shaking her head worriedly.

She did walk home from school with Sue, however, but when Sue asked anxiously, "What's the matter, Katie? Why are you acting so funny?" Katie declared, "Nothing's the matter. Who's funny? You're funny, that's who!" She started tickling Sue to make her laugh, and then the girls tickled and laughed and chased each other all the way home.

Over the weekend Katie John kept up her breeze and swagger, secretly noticing and relishing the puzzled looks her parents kept giving each other over her head. She did her household chores in a sloppy fashion and spent a good deal of time on her old trapeze in the mulberry tree. She also developed a rolling walk that involved much swinging of her arms.

Late Saturday she went down to the basement to watch her father, who was getting the furnace ready to turn on for the winter. It was a big old monster of a furnace, necessary to heat such a large house. With a shovel Dad removed clinkers, hard leftovers of coal that hadn't burned, and put them in a bucket Katie brought for him, muttering at himself for not doing this job last spring. It was sooty work, with the stirred-up ashes floating about, and Dad kept sneezing. To add to his troubles, the furnace door kept swinging shut against him as he leaned into the furnace to scoop at clinkers in the back.

"Here, hold the door open," he told Katie.

He leaned halfway into the furnace, dragged out a shovelful of clinkers, stepped back, and tripped over the bucket. The shovel load of clinkers went clanging over the cement floor, more clinkers spilled out of the bucket, and Dad fell in the middle of it all.

Sprawling on his back, Dad shouted, "These —" he took a deep breath "*CLINKERS!*"

Katie John admired the wealth of feeling in the word. It made a nice, satisfying ring. Dad looked as though he felt better too.

"Dad, when will I be old enough to swear?"

"Never!" Dad yelled. "What a question to ask at a time like this!"

Groaning and dusting himself off, Dad got up. "What do you mean, swear?" he asked. "With the greatest effort of self-control, I did *not* swear. Let this incident be a shining lesson in self-control, young lady," he added, getting back his good humor.

However, the value that Katie John gained from the incident was that "clinkers" made a wonderful explosion word. She didn't really want to swear, but she did want to sound rough and gruff in her new anti-girl, anti*little*-life role. For the rest of the weekend she went around shouting "*CLINKERS!*" whenever she wanted to let off steam or dropped a dish. Dad held his head and said he wished he'd never heard of clinkers, that he wished furnaces had never been invented, that he wished Katie would go read like a good little girl, that he wished Monday and schooltime would hurry up and come.

When Monday came, Katie John managed, by coming to the breakfast table with her coat on, to get out of the house without Mother seeing that she had her "bum" costume on again — the holey sweater and the old rumpled skirt.

At school the girls had on fresh, Monday-morning dresses, Howard and the boys were busy playing football before school, and Edwin didn't look at her at all when he sat down in his seat at the start of class. Katie John felt a pang. Everybody was going about his or her business, while she — what was she doing? Being different, she told herself firmly.

During class she cut out a circle of red paper and pinned it over the hole in her sweater. At morning recess Sue asked what the red circle was for.

"That's my spare belly button."

"Honestly, Katie John! You're awful!"

As a matter of fact, Katie John had felt awful as soon as she'd said it, but she wasn't going to admit it.

"Want me to make you a spare belly button?"

The worried lines in Sue's face smoothed into decision. "Katie John, I don't know why you're acting so strangely, but you're my friend and I'm going to tell you something. You're being just plain vulgar!

"And another thing," Sue went right on. "Why have you got that awful old sweater and skirt on? Don't you know what day this is? This is the day our sextet sings for the PTA program."

Oh, heavens! Katie had forgotten all about that.

She'd look like a bum standing with the other girls in their pretty dresses. She thought wildly of running home at noon to change clothes; she might have time enough if she went without lunch. But wait — wasn't that giving in, acting like all the rest of the girls, thinking clothes made such a difference? "So what if you do have old clothes on," she told herself. "What do you care about clothes? You don't want to be a dumb sweetly sweet girl anyway."

Through the rest of the morning a battle went on inside Katie John: "You wanted to be different; here's your chance. But I'll stick out like a sore thumb; a person wants to look decent in public." Oh, what was the matter with her? It used to be that she knew what she wanted to do, and then she did it — as simple as that. Now she didn't know whether she was going to run home at noon or not.

At lunchtime the singing teacher put an end to Katie's indecision. As soon as class was over, she rounded up the girls for a last rehearsal. There'd be no time at all to run home. The teacher was too intent on getting the girls to fit their voices together to notice what Katie was wearing. "That's right," Katie told herself, "the music is the important thing." She tried to concentrate on singing, "At the bend of the river—"

Just the same, she was still different. Just because of a little thing like a PTA program she wasn't going to go all stupid and girly-girl. Through the afternoon Katie John amused herself and the class with a large wad of bubble gum. The thing, of course, was to blow as large a bubble as possible without Mr. Boyle seeing her. Whenever his back was turned or his head was bent over papers at his desk, Katie started a bubble that grew and grew on her lips, to the fascination of the students in the adjoining seats. Always, at the last moment before the teacher turned around, she sucked the bubble in. Sammy, behind her, muttered eagerly that the bubble was going to blow up all over her face, but it never did.

After school, the six girls gathered in the rest room for last-minute hair combing before the PTA meeting began, and Katie's stomach was suddenly rather nervous, despite what her brain told her — that it was just a silly program, soon over. She threw away her red-paper spare belly button and used its pin to close the hole in her sweater. "There now," her brain told her stomach, "we're not going to worry one bit more about clothes." Then she forgot all about her appearance when she saw what Priscilla Simmons had in her hand.

Priscilla had a lipstick.

"Are you going to *wear* that?" Katie John exclaimed.

"What do you think I'm going to do, carry it like a torch?" Priscilla said pertly.

Leaning close to the mirror, she pulled her lips tight and spread the pale-pink lipstick over them. She bit her lips together and blotted them with tissue. There was no denying it, Priscilla looked even prettier with lipstick on.

"Oh, you look darling!" Betsy Ann said. "Priscilla, please, may I try it?"

Priscilla handed over the tube, and both Betsy Ann and Carole Jo applied slightly crooked pink mouths. It wasn't an awful red, just a soft pink. . . . Katie John drew closer, then suddenly stopped herself.

"Oh, ugh!" She made her voice disgusted. Chomping on her mouthful of bubble gum, she popped the wad loudly. "Aren't we sweet!"

The singing teacher called at the door for the girls to come; it was time to sing. "And remember, girls, open your mouths wide. Let the song come out."

"Okay, everybody. All got your spare belly buttons? Let's go." Katie John swaggered out the door in her rolling walk, arms swinging.

But she couldn't get the thought of that lipstick out of her mind. It was such a lovely color, and it did look pretty on Priscilla. The girls crowded into the small area offstage, waiting their turn to go onto the platform. As Priscilla put her little purse on a chair, Katie whispered to her, "Let me see your lipstick."

Priscilla took the tube from her purse and handed it to Katie. Forgetting the girls, Katie John gazed at the soft pink of the stick. She touched it with a gentle finger. So smooth. And such a nice pink, like a wild rose — but it didn't smell like a rose. . . . She sniffed again — more spicy, like carnations. . . . Oh, what was she doing, going all girly-sweet over a lipstick!

Pulling herself back to her breezy manner, she whispered to Priscilla, "It smells good enough to eat. What's it taste like?"

"It isn't for eating," Priscilla began, then stopped in dismay. For Katie John had bitten off the end of the lipstick and was chewing it.

"Katie John, you stop that!" Priscilla whispered fiercely, snatching back the tube. "That's my new lipstick that my mother gave me!"

"Never mind, it doesn't taste good at all," Katie mumbled around her mouthful, grinning.

As a matter of fact, she'd forgotten the bubble gum in her mouth, and now she had a horrid mixture. Bits of the lipstick had joined the gum, and the whole glob was crunchy and oily. Just as she reached up to take it from her mouth, Carole Jo shoved her toward the stage.

"Go on!" she said. "We're going onstage!"

Priscilla had already followed the file, and Katie stumbled after her onto the platform with the glob still in her mouth. The stage was brightly lit, rows and rows of mothers and small children spread below it. Oh, goodness, there was Mother, smiling at her. The piano music began. Heavens, how could she sing with this mess in her mouth? Would it be possible to swallow this much bubble gum — and lipstick? Katie tried to swallow and gagged. Oh dear, it was time to sing! She had to do something!

Swiftly she palmed the wad out of her mouth and clasped it between her hands in front of her, hands held in the approved fashion for singing.

"By the bend of the river . . ." she sang. Her mouth still felt oily and flecked with lipstick chips. The gum in her hand was slimy with saliva and chewed-up lipstick. A little of the slime oozed between her fingers — oh, could the audience see? Katie's voice shook. "S-so softly to m-me."

The song ended, the audience applauded, and then in sudden panic Katie John remembered the procedure for the next song. It was a country tune, and all the girls were to join hands and swing them gaily as they sang. Priscilla was on one side of her, Carole Jo on the other. What could she do with the mess in her hand? If she dropped it on the floor, the whole audience would see it, and some little kid in the front row would squawk about it. Besides, with her luck, she'd be sure to step in it. What? What? Where? Where? The music was beginning!

Fast as a hummingbird, Katie John dropped the dripping wad down inside the front of her sweater. "Stick!" she willed it. Unfortunately, her sweater wasn't tucked into her skirt. The wad tumbled down the front of her, and Katie caught it just as it fell out. Sure enough, that beady-eyed little kid down front snickered.

And just then Priscilla grabbed her hand to swing it gaily. "Toor-a-lay," Priscilla sang automatically, her lip lifted in disgust as she stared at her own and Katie's hands, then up at Katie. Katie held on tight, swinging away. "Liddle-day!" she trilled, scowling at Priscilla. She knew what would happen —

Too late! Priscilla wrenched her hand loose in strength made of horror. "What does she think I've got in my hand, a squashed mouse?" The thought fleeted in the midst of Katie's despair. And as the girls' hands flew apart, long dripping strings of gum clung to both their palms.

"Whoop!" squawked that kid down in front. A ripple of laughter spread over the audience as Katie frantically tried to gather up the strings of gum. Her mouth kept opening and shutting with the "liddle-days" as she wadded the glob up into both her hands and clasped them in front of her. Priscilla had stopped singing entirely, her face blank with shock as she stared at the gum hanging from her hand. The other girls continued to swing their arms and craned forward to look at Katie and Priscilla. One mother gave a high, uncontrolled titter, and then the whole audience was laughing out loud. ". . . on a lovely summer day!" the sextet struggled to the end of the song and rushed offstage amidst a thunder of applause and laughter.

Backstage, the girls began angrily:

"Katie John Tucker!"

"What on earth —"

"Honestly, Katie John!"

Face stiff, Katie pulled away from them. She ran down the deserted hallway, out a back door, ran until she came to a trash barrel set by the school wall. Fiercely she scraped and pulled the streamers of gum from her hands.

"I'll never chew gum again!" she gasped. "All those people! Laughing!"

How horrible! Horrible, horrible, horrible! Shudders began inside of her, and then she burst into tears, still pulling at the gum. She tried to be so smart and different, so antigirl, and all she'd done was ruin the program and make a big fool of herself. Oh, wouldn't this gum ever come off? She scraped her hand furiously on the metal barrel, hurting her hand, hating her hand, glad to hurt it.

Katie sank down on the sidewalk by the barrel and buried her head in her arms as she sobbed. A fool! That's what she was. That's what she'd been doing ever since last Friday, making a great big vulgar fool of herself. How could anyone ever want to speak to her again?

A Lady for a Day

KATIE COASTED. Looking back, she felt as if she'd been possessed by a demon, and now she was pale, purged, quiet: a convalescing invalid. When the girls in the rest room — naturally — brought up the subject of the gum Tuesday morning, Katie John only said, "I know," and withdrew to class. Seeing Katie so crushed and listless as the week progressed, Sue tried to be very kind to her friend, and Katie John was grateful. The other boys and girls steered clear of her, put off by her strange behavior — first so rowdy, now so quiet. Priscilla wouldn't even speak to her.

"Well, I got what I wanted," Katie John thought as she practiced penmanship. "I'm different, all right. I'm so different and out of step with everyone else that nobody likes me. Except Sue, of course." And she didn't really want to be different, Katie realized. It was just that — that she didn't want to be all silly and boy-chasing like most of the girls. She didn't want to be different from the girls; she wanted them to be like her. No, that wasn't it — how could she be her own self if all the other girls were duplicate Katie Johns?

Oh, she didn't know what she wanted, except not all this trouble. She wished she were back in the old days when the only trouble she got into was dropping curtains on renters' heads and chasing chickens with rotten eggs. Not all this tangle of how to act and how to get along with people. She glanced at Edwin's profile bent over his penmanship paper.

Had Netta, with her snub nose and freckles, had all this trouble in growing up?

Suddenly Katie remembered the Gypsy fortuneteller at the Street Fair and her predictions. The jack of hearts and a shovel, buried treasure. Edwin certainly was finding buried treasure at the deserted farm: all the clues to Netta. And the clues didn't even matter to him the way they did to Katie. But the pitchfork? Where did it come in? There wasn't any pitchfork in all this snarl. Katie John shook her head impatiently. It was all too complicated for her. Besides, fortunetelling was just a lot of foolishness.

The nights were chilly now. Friday evening Katie John carried firewood up to Miss Howell's apartment and watched the teacher start a blaze in her fireplace. As the kindling flames settled down to burning away the logs, Katie began telling Miss Howell how stupid the girls were acting these days with their boy-chasing.

Miss Howell looked up from the mitten she was knitting. "Katie John, tell me, what is it about the girls that bothers you so?"

"I just told you — how dumb they're acting."

"Yes dear, but what has that to do with you?"

Katie John poked some sticks against a glowing log.

She'd expected her beloved teacher to go "tch-tch" and be sympathetic, not analyzing and questioning.

"I don't want to be different," Katie said finally. "Is that how you have to act to grow up?"

Miss Howell laughed a brisk, friendly chuckle. "Nonsense, Katie, let the girls act as they like. Be yourself."

"But I don't even know who is myself any more," Katie John confessed unhappily.

Miss Howell picked at a dropped stitch. The fire popped in the silence. "I see you're past easy answers," she murmured. "Well, my dear, that search for 'who am I?' sometimes takes a person all her life."

"Some help!" Katie John snorted.

"Ah, Katie, cheer up." The teacher smiled at her. "I can tell you this: if you're honest with yourself, you'll know as much as you need to know at the right times."

Katie John shrugged and poked at the fire some more. This conversation was getting too grown-up for her. She didn't want to set out on some mysterious life-long search; she simply wanted to know how to fit in at school without all this silly boy-chasing.

"Well — thanks, Miss Howell, I'd better go now." She saw that the teacher had some papers laid out for correcting, and Mother had warned her not to take up too much of Miss Howell's time of an evening.

Katie John walked down the stairs, not ti-skip, ti-skip, the way she usually did. Instead her feet went ta-flat, ta-flat on each step. She wandered into the parlor. Now what to do? The Tuckers couldn't afford a television set yet — Katie suspected her father didn't even want one, the way he kept putting it off — and she'd read all of her library books. Checkers? No — Dad was off typing in a burst of evening work on his book, and Mother was mending at the sewing machine in the dining room. Except for the distant clack of Dad's typewriter and the stop-start whirs of the sewing machine, the house was quiet. Sometimes it was lonely, being an only child.

Looking for something to read, Katie John opened the glass doors of the ceiling-high bookcase. It was a very old piece of furniture left over from her great-grandfather's day, as were many of the books in it: a set of the encyclopedia, with the leather sloughing off the brown bindings; several dark volumes on the life of Napoleon; a set of the works of Washington Irving, big books and pamphlet-thin books crammed shelf-full, lying on top of each other, lined up two deep on the bottom shelf. Katie loved the smell of old paper that came from the bookcase. She pulled out a book at random, opened it, and sniffed the yellow pages — the dry old smell that stood for, promised . . . what? Delights, possibilities not yet known? Words that had been here all along, waiting for her? It was here that she'd found the book of pictures of Gibson Girls. Surely in all this wealth of books there must be something good to read.

600 Receipts, Church's Story of the Iliad, Two Years Before the Mast. That might be interesting. Katie John reached up to the book, and then her heart thumped. On the back binding of the book next to it was a picture, a drawing of a young woman with a bicycle and a perky feather in her hat. The girl looked as Katie had imagined Netta, setting out for bicycling. *Ladies' Home Manual of Physical Culture and Beauty,* read the title.

Katie John took the book down. On the front cover was another drawing, of a lady and two children gathering flowers. One of the children had a hoop and a stick for rolling it. Goodness, this must be an old book. She looked on the copyright page for the date of publication: 1896. Then Netta might have read just exactly this book of advice to ladies when she was growing up. Katie's heart beat a little faster as she opened the book. The pages parted at a picture of a woman with a fan, the picture titled, "A Moorish Beauty." Her fan was something like Netta's, but she certainly was much more romantic-looking than Netta. The beauty in the flowered robe had lovely dark eyes, graceful arms, and a dreamy look on her face that was nothing like Netta's open, cheerful face.

Katie John leafed through the book: "Advice to the Unmarried," "Teething," "Restoration of the Hair." It didn't seem very interesting. She flipped back through the pages again, and her eye was caught by a paragraph title: "Graceful Walking an Accomplishment." On the opposite page was a title, "Awkward Postures."

"Attitude, the simple pose of the body," Katie read, "is a matter of great importance. It reveals character and breeding." And farther down the page: "The true lady stands quietly on both legs . . . the toes turn out neatly." Katie giggled at the thought of women neatly pointing out their toes. "The arms hang naturally from the shoulders; the hands are in some quiet position, the fingers curve gracefully, with slight partings between the first and second, and the third and fourth."

Katie John skipped through this chapter on "Deportment and Manners," reading here and there with amusement: "It is now permitted to lean back when sitting. . . . Never stretch out the legs or spread them apart. . . . Long walks are too exhausting for much brainwork . . . No one has the right to offend others by appearing in public in dirty, disorderly, or unbecoming costume. . . . It is not delicate to scratch oneself. In public one may not comb her hair, clean her nails, spit, blow her nose or touch her nose or ears. . . . Never hum or whistle unless quite alone. Beware of sniffing. . . . Table conversation should be light, so as not to tax the brain while the life forces are gathered to the stomach. . . . 'If you please' is constantly on the lips of the Frenchman."

The book had a great deal to say about the attire and nature of a lady: "The rose in her hair is part of her womanhood. . . . Ringlets and frizzes hanging about the forehead suit almost everyone. . . . The parasol must be regarded as a kind of hat, a covering for the head." A lady, said the book, had "a sunny disposition, serene gaiety, a sweet, engaging manner." She was "punctual, orderly, dependable; one can trust her utterly."

"The lady who boasts becomes ridiculous." Katie John read this uncomfortably. "Avoid slang such as 'awfully nice.' Say 'I thank you,' not 'thanks.' Avoid exclamations and exaggerations. . . . The hoyden is defined to be a rude, rough, romping girl." Oh, oh! The book could have been talking about her, the way she'd been acting.

So this was how Netta had to behave to be a lady, a proper maiden. Katie John liked the word "maiden"; it sounded like the olden times. How had that merry-faced girl ever managed to fit into all this?

And then Katie John had a good idea. Why not try following these rules just for a day, to see what Netta had to go through? It would be fun. Yes, that was just exactly what she was going to do. All day tomorrow she'd be a lady, a proper maiden. Katie John went through the book again, laughing and shaking her head, studying the rules and advice that she wanted to follow. Then she went to bed early to lie there and plan what she'd do.

The last thing Katie remembered before falling asleep was to close her mouth so she wouldn't snore, according to the *Ladies' Home Manual* rules. And she must be careful what she dreamed. The book said, "One must not even *dream* an impropriety." You couldn't even be unladylike in your dreams.

Then Katie John dreamed of squatty green ogres chasing pretty maidens. And Little Miss Muffet sat on a tuffet, picking her nose in public. Along came Sammy Spider and sat down beside her . . . and Priscilla sailed up in her swan boat, not even leaning back, her toes pointed out neatly. "See what a lady I am?" she said, and then she gunned her swan boat after Howard, who was riding a caterpillar. Next,

Katie John was jumping rope, yelling, "I hate the boys and they hate me-e-e. I'd rather be a girl than act re-pul-sivel-lyyy!" while all the girls stood around counting, "Two hundred, two hundred one, two hundred two . . ."

Katie John awoke in the morning not at all exhausted, but eager to get at her "lady" role.

"It's about time I tried to be a lady," she said firmly, with her dreams still hazy in her mind.

The first thing she did was to brush her hair until it clung in a smooth shape. Then, awkwardly, she wound her bangs in pin curls so that later in the day she'd have "ringlets hanging about her forehead." Dressed in a fresh blouse and skirt, she stood with her back against the wall, according to instruction in the *Manual*, and walked away, back straight, head erect. No, she was forgetting to turn out her toes. Katie returned to the wall, lined her back up against it, got her toes pointed out properly, and walked away again. Her head felt high, and pointing her toes out made her stomach tend to stick out. She pulled it in, keeping her back straight, and then forgot to breathe. At last she got everything coordinated. Walking like this made her feel like an old lady. She'd seen some of them in the neighborhood walking this way, as if they weren't really going anywhere.

Oh yes, one other thing: her fingers should curve gracefully — how was it? Katie found the place in the *Ladies' Home Manual*, which she'd put on her bedstand. "The fingers curve gracefully, with slight partings between the first and second, and the third and fourth." She got the fingers on her right hand organized, then her left hand. It was easy once she remembered to keep the middle fingers together. Her fingers felt stiff though, not at all graceful in their curves.

However, off we go. Back straight, head erect (so that she couldn't see the floor), middle fingers together, toes pointed out neatly, Katie John approached the breakfast table. Unfortunately, no one noticed her. Dad was behind his newspaper, and Mother was dishing up scrambled eggs at the stove.

"Here, give this to your father." Mrs. Tucker handed Katie a plate of eggs.

Katie John tried to curve her parted fingers gracefully around the plate and almost dropped it. She settled for continuing to walk erectly, toes out, with the result that she felt like a court page bringing forward milord's crown on a satin cushion. She set the eggs down between Dad and his paper. Dad only grunted.

From noon on, Dad was a wonderfully jolly father, witty, interested in other people. But the first thing in the morning he was silent, eyes glazed, taking his time at waking up, not really a part of this world yet. And right after breakfast he always disappeared into the front bedroom to write on his second mystery book.

Mother, however, was always awake in the morning. The *Manual* said a person should make only light conversation at the table, so Katie John chattered away to Mother about how nicely the birds were singing this morning, and how long would it be before all the robins were gone.

Dad frowned over the top of his paper at her. "Quiet down." To Mother he said, "That reminds me. *Must* you have those women here for tea this afternoon?"

Readily, Katie quoted the *Manual:* " 'Table conversation should be light, so as not to tax the brain when the life forces are gathered to the stomach.' "

Dad growled, "My life forces are just getting organized for the day, and they need silence."

He began to eat his eggs and added to Mother, "These eggs are watery."

" 'Never mention food at the table,' " his daughter instructed him. " 'What one is fond of may disgust another.' "

Dad's eyes came unglazed as he glowered at her. "Just who are you trying to be today?"

With dignity, curling her fingers gracefully around her toast, Katie replied, "I am *trying* to be a lady."

Then she recalled the book: "Haughty manners are the language of pride," so she smiled at her father in a sweet, engaging manner, with a sunny disposition, with serene gaiety.

Dad retired behind his newspaper muttering, "I don't think I'm going to like it."

Through the rest of breakfast Lady Katie contented herself with saying, "If you please" and "I thank you," until even Mother stared at her. Noticing Katie's clothing, she told her not to wear her school things for doing housework this morning.

"Wear them this afternoon when you may help me serve at the tea party," she suggested.

For once Katie John was delighted to be included in

the gathering of a few women from the neighborhood. A tea party would be just the place to try out her ladylike accomplishments. By afternoon she expected to have them perfected. Besides, Netta might often have had to help with tea parties when she'd rather be out bicycling.

After breakfast she changed her clothes, but she didn't mind, for she'd had another good idea. She should wear a long skirt to help her move like a lady. In jeans you didn't feel ladylike; in jeans it was natural to throw your legs around. But in a long skirt she'd flow about the rooms at her work. Katie John ran up the back stairs to Great-aunt Emily's trunk on the third-floor landing and dug around in it. She knew better than to take one of the nice skirts, but here was just the thing, a long white flannel petticoat with a flounce around the bottom. She folded it over once at the waist to take it up off the floor and fastened the hooks. Now she was ready to wash dishes in true lady-like fashion.

When she got back to the kitchen, Mother was putting into the oven a loaf of nut bread that she'd made before breakfast. She'd prepared the cookies and other dainties for the tea yesterday.

"This is to come out in fifty minutes," she told Katie. "You keep an eye on the clock and take it out in case I'm still upstairs cleaning Mr. Watkins' room."

After Katie washed the dishes, she was to dust the parlor — carefully! — and then Mrs. Tucker would vacuum the room.

She broke off in the midst of her instructions at the

sight of Katie's petticoat. Before she could say anything, Katie explained that it was to help her to feel like a lady. Mother's lips twitched, and then she shrugged and went out, smiling.

Now everyone was sorted out to his day's duties: Dad at his typewriter in the front bedroom, Mother upstairs with the scrub bucket and clean sheets, Katie John at the kitchen sink.

Instead of running down the stairs, she'd held the petticoat up off the steps and taken one step at a time. Now she tied an apron over it and moved slowly, sweetly, gently, as she cleared the kitchen table. The long skirt swished about her legs agreeably. No wonder women were so proper in the olden days; the drape of the skirts practically forced you to float like a swan. A fold caught between Katie's legs, and she kicked it out before she remembered. Oh dear, she was forgetting to keep her back straight and point out her toes too. So many things to remember.

It was easier when she was simply standing at the sink washing dishes. After a time, however, she discovered that washing dishes as a lady was no different from washing dishes as Katie John. It was the same old business: scrape off the egg and rinse the plate. Nothing ladylike involved there. Ladylike behavior must be mostly connected with how you act around other people, she decided. Still, she could think ladylike thoughts. What did maidens think about? Swains, new plumed hats, what to wear to the ball tonight? Hm, oh — boys and clothes, the same as the girls at school now, if that were true. What would Netta have thought about? That she'd rather be out bicycling on such a lovely autumn morning? "That's no different from me," Katie thought. Well, then, what would ladies think about? Loaves of bread to be baked, baskets for the poor, grocery lists? Katie's mind went blank. She couldn't think of any interesting ladylike thoughts to think. So she sang. "By the bend of the river . . ."

As she dusted in the parlor, she continued to sing sweetly, skirt swishing, toes pointed out as she moved about the room. The petticoat pouffed out on the floor when she knelt to wipe the bends in the legs of the little center table. Carefully she dusted, picking up every vase and ornament left over from Great-aunt Emily's day. And there was a multitude of them — big cloisonné bowls on top of the piano, black iron urns on the mantel, Chinese pots on the whatnot, and in between a scattering of vases of all shapes and sizes. Dad said the place looked as cluttered as a dime store, but Mother said she rather liked it. She could say that; it was Katie's weekly duty to dust them.

Then Katie John had another good idea. Wouldn't the parlor look lovely for the tea party if all the vases had flowers in them? Petticoat whipping between her legs, she ran outdoors to see what flowers were left in the garden. It being the middle of October, there weren't many, but Katie John gathered all the last yellow roses and the little button chrysanthemums, wishing she had a floppy hat and a flower basket on her arm, as in the pictures of maidens she'd seen. She made another trip for an armload of bright maple leaves. The gold and bronze leaves made a splendid display massed in the blue bowls on the piano —"the very colors of autumn," Katie John thought happily, "the blue of the bowls the same shade as today's sky."

" 'Twas the last ro-ose uh-of sum-mer," she trilled as she arranged the roses in some of the vases. In others she clustered the chrysanthemums. More leaves for the mantel urns, a single yellow rose in a bud vase, three orange button mums for the fat little Chinese vase on its three legs. When Katie John was done, everything in the room that could hold flowers held them, even if only two or three. She got water from the kitchen — my, that nut bread smelled good! — and watered all the flowers and leaves. She was just wiping up the dribbles when Mother came running downstairs.

"Katie John, I can smell that nut bread clear up on the third floor! Haven't you taken it out yet?"

Oh heavens, the nut bread had been in the oven over an hour and a half. Absorbed in the flowers, she'd forgotten the time. Mrs. Tucker pulled the pan out of the oven.

"Well, it's certainly done! It'll be as hard as a rock. Katherine John Tucker! Honestly!"

Katie John remembered the *Ladies' Home Manual*: "A lady is dependable. You can trust her utterly."

"I'm sorry. Could I make some more?"

Mother threw up her hands. "You don't know how. Never mind."

To make up for it, Katie John offered to vacuum the parlor, promising to do such a good job that sharp old Miss Crackenberry would never spy a thread on the carpet.

And so the morning passed. After a quick lunch, Dad

escaped the house for the afternoon, and Mrs. Tucker and Katie laid out the tea things on the dining-room table, nicely in view of the parlor through the open folding doors. Despite the nut-bread flurry, Katie John still felt sweet and gracious. By now she thought she had quite the hang of pointing out her toes and curving her fingers and speaking softly. She took a maidenly pleasure at the sight of the tea table, silver gleaming, little cakes and cookies arranged on crystal or old hand-painted china plates, dainty spoons lined up. Mother had decided to use some of the nut bread, after all, even though it was pretty hard. At least it didn't crumble when Katie John buttered it.

Now all was ready, and two thirty was approaching. Time for tea with the ladies! Katie John retired to her room to dress. First she took Netta's fan from the drawer that she'd pushed it into. Holding it in her hands, she considered carrying it with her, then decided she didn't quite have the nerve. Still, she hung it back on its nail over her bed. Then she put on her best dress and took the pins out of her bangs. Now for the ringlets.

But, oh dear, the ends hadn't curled. She had a waving mass on her forehead, but all the ends were straight spikes. She'd never pinned curls before, and now look! Katie brushed and brushed, but the spikes just would go every which way. At last she gave up. Anyway, the rest of her looked all right. Katie John lined her back up against the wall, got her middle fingers together, and moved off to the tea party.

Sue Halsey's mother and another mother-aged woman had already arrived. They were exclaiming to

Mrs. Tucker about how pretty the parlor looked with all the flowers.

"We have Katie John to thank," Mother said, giving her daughter a rather strange look.

Katie saw that some of the vases didn't have flowers in them now, however. Mother must have come into the parlor for a last look at the room before the party and taken some away. Why? The parlor had been a regular bower of flowers before. Oh well, there were still plenty. Katie John smiled modestly and said, "I thank you," when Mrs. Halsey complimented her on the arrangement of the leaves. Now Miss Crackenberry arrived with another old neighbor lady named Mrs. Lovell, and Mother sat at the tea table to pour. Katie John stood back, curving her fingers.

Soon everyone was seated in the parlor, chatting about the delightful weather and balancing teacups on plates full of dainties. Katie John had tea, too, generously diluted with cream. She'd managed to get it to the parlor and sit down without spilling any. Heavens, here was something else that *forced* you to move smoothly. She didn't like the milky tea, so she drank it down quickly to get rid of it, then ate her cookies. Too late she realized that the other ladies were only sipping their tea. She was the only one with an empty cup and plate. She thought of going back to the tea table for more, but realized that would make her look greedy. So she set the plate on a table beside her and folded her hands in her lap.

"What interesting nut bread. Quite different," said old Mrs. Lovell.

Katie John noticed that she laid the nut bread on

her plate after one bite and didn't touch it again. Katie John didn't think that was really very polite. Mrs. Lovell was the oldest one there, and she should know the most about manners. Mrs. Lovell had white hair, brown spots on her face, and her chin shook slightly with a continual palsy. Her thin old legs stuck out in front of her like sticks from under her black skirts.

After Katie had seen all there was to see about Mrs. Lovell, she tried listening to the conversation. The ladies were talking about someone who'd broken her hip. Why did women always talk about illnesses and operations? So boring. Presently Katie John began to itch. It was a spot right in the middle of her back, which of course she mustn't reach for. Her finger strayed up to rub her nose, but she remembered in time. A lady never scratched or touched her nose in public. The spikes of her "ringlets" tickled her forehead, but Katie John clenched her hands in her lap. Now that scratching was impossible, more and more itchy spots began to twitch — her neck, her ear, her leg — but Katie John was a lady. Grimly she bore the torture, and at last the itchings went away. Then before she realized it, she found she was nibbling on a fingernail. Gracious! She put the offending finger down and looked at the other ladies. No wonder women sipped tea and ate cakes at tea parties. The business gave them something to do with their hands.

What a tremendous amount of self-control it took simply to sit, not moving your hands, not touching yourself, not doing anything. Had Netta ever learned to do this?

Now Miss Crackenberry in the next chair was saying

something to her. "How do you like school, Katherine John?" she said in the polite way that old people have when they decide to talk to a child.

School? Awful boys, boy-chasing girls. "Fine, thanks," Katie John replied, then changed it to, "I mean, it is lovely, I thank you. And how is your work, Miss Crackenberry?"

The old lady looked at her sharply, and Katie John remembered the *Manual* rule to look the speaker clearly in the eye while listening.

"Young lady, are you being impertinent?"

"My goodness, no!" (One shouldn't use exclamations.) "I mean, I'm sorry if I seemed to be, Miss Crackenberry."

"Hmph. My housework is as usual."

Mother was going about refilling the ladies' teacups now, and she asked Katie John to pass the cookie plate.

As she went out, Mrs. Halsey was saying, "I almost ran into General Pomfroy today."

The statue of Barton Bluff's Civil War hero stood right in the way of cars, in the middle of the intersection at Third and Main Streets. When Katie came back with the plate of cookies, Miss Crackenberry was talking about the statue. It seemed that Barton's Bluff had long ago acquired the cast for the statue from the state government, as the original stood with other statues at the state capital — something Katie John hadn't known before. Well, now, for once the ladies were talking about something interesting.

"Never saw a town act so foolish," Miss Crackenberry said. "First they couldn't decide to buy the cast.

Then, when General Pomfroy was delivered, they couldn't decide where to put him. Some wanted him in the park, some wanted him at the top of Main Street, some wanted him down here closer to the river, where they finally put him. And then when they decided that, they fought about which way he'd face, toward the Mississippi or west toward the town. People! They took sides — General Pomfroy facing east, and General Pomfroy west. Letters to the editor, indignation meetings — bosh! A lot of nonsense!"

"Yes, it certainly was a lot of nonsense," Mrs. Lovell said, her chin shaking. "I always did think poor old General Pomfroy would rather have faced the river. It bothers me every time I pass him."

Katie John giggled. Mrs. Lovell looked at her, and she remembered the *Ladies Home Manual* said, "You cannot laugh without explaining what you are laughing at." But how could she explain that she was laughing at Mrs. Lovell?

Lamely she said, "Oh yes, it certainly was nonsense."

Turning to Miss Crackenberry, she saw a gleam in the old eyes. Would wonders never cease? Was that a smile moving on those thin, dry lips? It was gone too soon to tell. Katie held out the cookie plate to her, and Miss Crackenberry selected a nut-filled sand tart without an "I thank you."

Katie John curved the fingers of her free hand gracefully and prepared to float about the room with maidenly grace. Back straight, head high, she toed-out over to Mrs. Lovell with the cookie plate. But alas for high heads that can't see the floor — Katie John tripped.

Whoops! The cookies went flying off the plate. She tried to juggle them and catch herself, tangled in Mrs. Lovell's legs, and fell backward. One lone cookie remained on the plate. Stupidly, from the floor, Katie John went on with what she had been about to say:

"Mrs. Lovell, may I offer you a cookie?"

All the lovely little nut cookies and stuffed dates were scattered across Mrs. Lovell's lap, the couch, the floor. The ladies were exclaiming, Katie's feet were still tangled up with Mrs. Lovell's — it was too awful to contemplate. Katie John closed her eyes.

Unfortunately, she had to open them again. You can't simply disappear by closing your eyes, any more than the ostrich does when he puts his head in the sand.

She pulled her feet free from Mrs. Lovell's. If the old lady hadn't had them stuck out in such an unladylike way, she wouldn't have tripped, but maybe her legs were too old to bend easily.

"Did I hurt you?" Katie John worried, picking up the sand tarts from Mrs. Lovell's black dress.

Mrs. Lovell's chin shook even more, but she quavered that she was all right. "Don't worry, child." Mother was on her feet, helping to pick up the dates and cookies from the floor. Katie John stood uncertainly with the plate, not knowing what to do. Should she go on offering the cookies? Mother stopped her.

"We can't eat them now," she murmured, but her voice was kind. "Take them to the kitchen."

Mrs. Halsey's voice broke through the chatter, "Sue is home, and she was hoping you'd go bicycling with her this afternoon, Katie John."

The easy out — but to go in disgrace? Katie John looked at Mother questioningly.

Mother nodded. "Go ahead. And don't worry — accidents happen." She smiled. "If I were a good hostess now, I'd trip over Miss Crackenberry's legs to put you at ease. It's just too bad you didn't do it with the nut bread instead."

Grateful to Mother for making it easier for her, Katie John started for the kitchen with the cookie plate. Then at the folding doors she turned back.

In her most ladylike voice she said, "It's been so nice to see you all. Such a lovely afternoon. Good-bye."

To a chorus of good-byes, Katie John ran out to the kitchen. There she found Heavenly Spot looking hungry, so she fed him two of the cookies before she thought better of it. The sand tarts weren't really dirty. After all, most of them had fallen on Mrs. Lovell and the couch. Katie John put them in a paper sack to munch on with Sue.

Later the girls rode out along the River Road, where the autumn hills were a mass of glory against the sky. Katie John had told Sue about her Lady Katie day and its awful climax, concluding, "I get into trouble even when I *try* to be a lady." But now, with the red and gold hills on one side of her and the river flowing wide by the road, the blue sky overhead, and the sun warm on her back, Katie John thought of the scene in the parlor and laughed. That look on Mrs. Lovell's face when the sand tarts came scattering across her lap, and that one lone cookie on the plate — "Mrs. Lovell, may I offer you a cookie?" Katie John giggled. All in all, it had been fun being a lady for a day, but she was relieved it was over. What a strain to have to keep toeing out and saying "I thank you" forever. Poor Netta. She must have been glad to come out to live on a farm by the river.

Katie John gasped. "Look at *that* tree!"

She stopped her bike and stood looking at a small but especially beautiful maple tree that stood alone, taking in its flaming glory. Compelled, she dropped her bicycle at the roadside and climbed over the ditch to the maple. Scooping up some leaves from underneath it, she let them shower over her head and shoulders, holding some in her hands.

"Is this how it feels, tree?"

She stood, caught in the golden moment. Slowly she released one leaf from her hand to let it drift down, just as the maple tree slowly released its splendor each passing day of the autumn.

Finally Sue, watching from the road, broke the silence.

"You know, Katie John, that's what I like about you. Other people would say, 'Isn't that a pretty tree?' and go on. But you — you mix in. I don't know, but when you like a thing you do something about it. You live so much more than other people, Katie John."

Katie John smiled at her sister, the maple tree, and thought good-bye. Sue might be right, though she didn't understand exactly. But then, neither did Katie John. All she knew was that she'd rather do this than be a lady any day.

In Which Nothing Goes Wrong

RHODA PHILLIPS ASKED, "Are you going to have a Halloween party again this year?"

"Well sure — why not?" Katie John said. "If my mother will let me, I guess —"

"Hey, Sally!" The fat girl ran off down the school hallway. "Katie John's going to have another Halloween party!"

"If my mother will let me!" Katie called after her.

The idea worked and developed in Katie's mind during the school day. A Halloween party. Yes, it should be fun. And it would be a chance to get back on some kind of normal footing with the other girls, too. Last Halloween she and Sue had given a party at Katie's house, and everyone had had a wonderful time. Now, if Mother would only agree. Let's see, she'd invite Sue, of course, and Rhoda, since she'd started the idea, and Helen from the singing sextet, and she supposed she ought to ask Priscilla and her gang. And she'd ask Lou. Louisa Beauty was her real name, but she was a quiet little mouse — certainly no beauty — and everyone just called her Lou. Still, she got an interesting look on her face sometimes, and Katie John thought she'd like to know Lou better.

That made seven guests — oh, fiddle! She couldn't do that. Last Halloween all the girls in the class had been invited. She couldn't leave out some this year, for they might be hurt. No, if there was to be a party at all, everyone should be included.

On the way home from school, Katie John and Sue were full of chatter about the idea. There could be fortunetelling — they'd never forgotten the Gypsy at the Street Fair — and popcorn balls, and a tubful of apples in water to dunk for, and hide-and-seek in the dark, many-roomed cellar under Katie's house, and the girls could talk through the speaking tubes again.

The speaking tubes in the old house, a nineteenth-century version of an intercom system, were built into the walls, with round-hole openings in various rooms. In the olden days, Katie's Clark ancestors had used the tubes to talk to servants or other members of the family in distant rooms. Tricks with the speaking tubes had been a main feature of last year's Halloween party. Of course, this year the guests wouldn't be fooled, but at least they could have fun talking through the tubes.

Mother agreed to the party. "I'll help!" Katie promised. "I'll help with everything. You won't have to do hardly a thing!"

Then the girls rushed off to Katie's room to make invitations. On the outside of folded heavy paper they colored wicked orange jack-o'-lanterns. On the inside they printed:

> **THE WITCHES SUMMON YOU**
> *When:* The scariest night of the year
> *Where:* Katie John Witch's house
> *What time:* The witching hour (7:30 P.M.)
> *Why:* For fearful, frightening fun

Sue made an invitation for herself as a souvenir. Katie John finished the invitations she'd been working on and counted all they'd made. Yes, there were enough for all the girls in their room.

"Twelve," she said. "Twelve guests."

"No, thirteen," Sue said. "There'll be thirteen of us. You didn't make an invitation for yourself."

Thirteen! Thirteen at a Halloween party!

"Oh no-o," Katie John groaned. "We're jinxed right from the start. Something awful will happen!"

"Last year we had the same bunch, and everything went all right," Sue soothed her.

"That's right. . . . No, there must have been only twelve of us, because Helen was sick and couldn't come."

Katie John brooded. Every time she set out to do something interesting, every time she had a good idea, something went wrong — tripping over Mrs. Lovell's legs, the caterpillar ride at the Street Fair. Well, this party was *not* going to have any disasters. She'd simply *make* it go smoothly.

"Sue, I'm not going to be superstitious," Katie John

declared. "This party is going to be one time when nothing goes wrong. I vow!"

"Good." Sue laughed. "I wish you luck."

Next, the girls planned their costumes. Sue said she'd wear her witch's costume from last year. Katie John decided to rig up as a fortuneteller, for Sue insisted Katie should be the one to tell the fortunes. It was time for Sue to go home for supper, and the girls parted, agreeing to distribute the party invitations at school tomorrow.

Katie John was vaguely dissatisfied with the idea of dressing as a fortuneteller, however. This year she'd wanted to be something really horrible for Halloween. How could she make the Gypsy outfit more scary or mysterious? At the supper table she edged into the idea by asking Dad, who ought to have ideas from his mystery-story writing.

"I don't know whether to be a fortuneteller or not. That's not very horrible. What's the most horrible thing you can think of, Dad?"

"An evening with a houseful of squealing girls," Dad said. "Ho-ho for Halloween!"

Mother spoke thoughtfully. "You know, I think the most horrible thing would be a black ghost. White ghosts are common, but imagine seeing a black ghost in the fog, floating over the ground in a misty white field at night. Brrr."

Katie John had stopped eating mashed potatoes to look at her mother. You'd suppose all Mother ever thought about was making over dresses with Mrs. Halsey, yet here she'd come up with a piece of imagination that was truly wonderful. A black ghost! Katie John shivered.

"Oh, I like that! A wispy, wailing, black ghost!"

She must be a black ghost for the party. Still, what about the fortunetelling? Katie John was torn. But the idea of being a black ghost was too dramatic to resist. She'd simply tell fortunes as a ghost. After all, it wasn't everybody who had her fortune told by a black ghost.

"That's what I want to be," Katie John decided. "Mother, will you help me make the costume?"

As they did the supper dishes, she and Mother planned, and Katie John felt closer to her mother than she had in a long time. Mother said she'd dye an old sheet black for the basic costume, and Katie was to hunt through Aunt Emily's trunks for some long black mitts to cover her arms, which would stick out through holes in the sheet. Mother would fashion a kind of black hood to fit closely on Katie's head. Dad, who was still sitting at the kitchen table, listening, said he'd blacken Katie's face with burnt cork or charcoal.

"I'll be completely black," Katie John said with relish. "But I need more of a wispy effect. The sheet will float around my legs, but I need something more. I know: I'll sew long strips of black rags to my shoulders to swirl out — and straggles of rags to the hood on my head, too."

She could just see the black lines writhing from her head, blowing in a ghostly breeze. Ah! How satisfying!

The next day before school Katie and Sue passed out the party invitations. All the girls seemed eager for the party and free to come to it.

"Will there be boys at the party?" Betsy Ann asked.

"No!" Good night, what a thought!

"Of course not," Priscilla said. "Katie's a boy-hater."

Katie followed Priscilla's glance at Howard, who was leaning against the wall with his hands in his pockets, talking quietly enough, for once, to Edwin. The two boys were watching the group of girls around Katie John.

"That's right," some of the girls were saying. "Katie's the boy-hater."

Her reputation on that point seemed solid enough. Huh! As if she were an accepted freak on the subject. Katie muttered to herself, then stopped. Never mind that now. The important thing at hand was the Halloween party, and it was going to be fun. Mustn't let any other worries interfere with the party.

After school, Katie John and Sue went to Katie's room to plan the fortunetelling. Fortunes for all the girls would be written out on folded slips of paper, numbered, and put in a bowl. With the bowl on a small table before her, Katie John was to sit under the green-glass hanging lamp in the dining room. The old-fashioned chandelier had a green beaded fringe hanging down from its rim, and somehow it reminded the girls of a fortuneteller's nook. First Katie would read the palm of her "client's" hand. Then she would have the girl pick a card from a deck. The number on the card would be the number of her fortune.

Katie John sharpened pencils, and she and Sue set themselves to the fascinating business of figuring out fortunes.

"They should be something really different," Katie said. "Fortunes about tall dark men and journeys over water are too common. And they shouldn't be something that the girls can prove won't come true by the very next day. Like, don't say 'Tomorrow you will find a billfold.'"

Silence prevailed in Katie's room. Then the creative juices began to flow.

"You will be chased by a bat, but you will get away," Katie John wrote. After all, it could happen sometime in a girl's life. She wasn't saying when.

"You will receive a present smaller and better than you ever expected," Sue contributed. Some of the girls might get wrist watches for Christmas.

Katie John nudged her brain for something really out of this world. Oh, heavens. She sat up straight. That was an amazing idea!

"You will marry a man from another planet," she said. "How's that for a fortune!"

Sue looked half frightened. "What a thought!" She shuddered. "I hope I don't get that fortune."

The girls' ideas flowed on amidst giggles and flashes of inspiration: "Your tomcat will turn out to be a girl and have kittens." "You will grow up to be a raving beauty, and I do mean *raving*." "A witch will be watching you when you go home tonight, but you won't be able to see her." ("I hope Priscilla gets that one," Katie John muttered.) "You will rescue a squirrel with a wounded paw and make a pet of him." "Trouble lies in your near future unless you smile every day before breakfast." "You will perform on television and be a tremendous success." "A very strange visitor will come to your house. Beware!"

"Beware of what?" Sue questioned that one.

"Just 'beware!' That's to make it mysterious."

The girls finished writing the fortunes, folded the slips of paper, and put them in Katie's dresser drawer for safekeeping.

Katie John continued the party planning in the week that remained before Halloween. Of course Sue helped, but Katie John would be the hostess, and the final responsibility that nothing go wrong rested on her shoulders. Careful planning right down to the last detail was the key, she decided. She'd think it all through, anticipate every difficulty, and smooth it out beforehand. She planned exactly where the tubful of apples in water would be placed in the basement, so that no one would come running down the stairs in the dark and fall into it. She even checked the metal washtub to make sure it didn't leak — that was all they'd need, to come down and find all the water had leaked out on the cement floor.

She thought out the sequence of events for the party. There shouldn't be any dull spots of aimless milling around. First, the girls could talk through the speaking tubes to one another in different rooms. That way there'd be something to do as soon as a girl arrived — no waiting for everyone to come before the party could start. When everyone had arrived and admired one another's costumes and had had a chance at the speaking tubes, she'd start the fortunetelling. While each girl was having her fortune told, the rest, in two teams, could be passing an apple along under their chins. And if masks or costumes made apple passing hard, so much the more fun.

Next they'd all go down to the cellar and bob for apples. Let's see now: everyone couldn't bob for apples at once. What could the others be doing? Something in another dark room of the basement — aha! — spaghetti worms! Sue could supervise the apple bobbing while Katie sat in the coal cellar with a big bowlful of cold cooked spaghetti. The girls could come in one at a time, and she'd say, "This is a test of your courage," and she'd push the girl's hand into the cold spaghetti. "This is a bowlful of worms," she'd say, "and the one who eats the most gets a prize!" There ought to be plenty of shrieks out of that. Then she'd tell the girl that it was really spaghetti and make her promise not to tell the others who hadn't been in.

When all that was over, they'd play hide-and-seek in the basement with the lights out — that should be lots of scary fun — and then they'd go upstairs for refreshments. With her mother, Katie John planned the party food: popcorn balls, cookies with orange or black icing, little pumpkin tarts (Mother's idea), and orange punch. Katie was almost afraid to help with the preparation of the food for fear she'd do something awful to it, but Mother promised to check her on every step, working right alongside.

As to the other Halloween details, Mother and Dad agreed to answer the door to hand out cookies to the trick-or-treaters, so that Katie John would be free to run her party. Dad offered to carve the big pumpkins for the front porch and the centerpiece for the refreshment table, and a few small ones for dark corners of the cellar. He also got the burnt cork ready to smear on his daughter's face. The making of the black ghost costume went along without trouble. Katie John warned Mr. Watkins, the renter on the third floor, of the impending party and promised that the girls would stay off that floor so as not to disturb his sleep. Mr. Watkins was night watchman at the flour mill and usually slept during the early evening until time to go to work. However, the big man assured her solemnly that it was all right:

"On Halloween night I go to work early to protect."

And at last it was Halloween night. Katie John, the black ghost, surveyed herself in the mirror of the dining-room sideboard. Ah yes, she was truly, wonderfully, satisfyingly horrible. All black. When she moved, the black rags straggled out from her shoulders and head almost as well as she'd imagined. And her face under the black hood! That was a real triumph. Dad had blackened it with the cork, but better yet, Mother had produced a white lipstick she'd bought downtown. With it, she'd made the area around Katie's eyes a ghoulish white that stood out against the black of her face.

"Ooo-oo-ha-ha-a!" The black ghost gave a horrible chuckle at her image in the mirror.

Mother had gone to the kitchen to prepare a plate of cookies for the trick-or-treaters, but Dad stood around watching Katie and pretending to complain.

"Grownups never get to have any fun on Halloween.

Halloween's become a national holiday for children. Not fair. Grownups can think of lots more gruesome things to do than kids can. Hey, Abby!" he called to Mother. "Get your coffee cup and let's go trick-or-treating!"

Katie John whirled. "Daddy, don't you dare leave! You've got to answer the door —"

Then she saw that he was laughing, and she giggled nervously in turn. Dad made a show of settling grumpily with his evening paper, while Katie John ticked off details in her mind. All the jack-o'-lanterns were in place and the candles lit. The fortune papers were in the bowl on a little table under the green chandelier, with a chair on each side of the table. All the refreshments were ready and waiting. The party napkins and glasses were set out on the dining table, which looked quite festive with its huge pumpkin face and Halloween paper tablecloth. The apple tub was filled and in place in the basement, and the bowl of cooked spaghetti — oh, that was still in the kitchen. She'd better put it down in the coal cellar before the girls saw it.

As she started for the kitchen, the doorbell rang. Oh goodness, were the girls coming already, or was it a trick-or-treater? Katie John ran to the front door. On the front porch she found a small white ghost.

"I've come to the party," it announced.

Katie John recognized the voice emerging from under the rather soiled sheet. The voice belonged to a little boy from the next block.

"Sorry, Petie," Katie said firmly. "This party is just for girls."

She found a cookie for the ghost and sent him on his rounds.

Now to tend to that spaghetti before anything else happened. Katie John hurried to the kitchen. Where was the bowl?

"On the chair," Mother said, not looking up from working the pumpkin tarts out of the tart pans.

"Spot!" Katie John shrieked.

Heavenly Spot, that dear, agreeable, floppy-eared dog, had his paws up on the kitchen chair, his nose in the bowl of spaghetti.

"Mother! He's eating it! Oh, you bad dog, get away!"

Katie John grabbed up the bowl and saw with relief that about half the spaghetti was still left. Nothing had really gone wrong. There was still enough to seem like a mess of slimy worms. Just the same, she scolded her dog:

"You've had your supper. Don't you get enough to eat that you have to eat cold spaghetti? Shame on you!"

Heavenly Spot hung his head, but looked up out of the corner of one eye to see if he could have some more spaghetti.

"Come on now. You're going outdoors before you cause any more trouble."

Katie John put the beagle on the high back porch and then stood outside for a moment, her rags whipping in the wind, savoring the dark Halloween night. The sky was completely black — no moon, no stars — and the wind blew in fits and hurries, with strange quiet spaces between gusts. Now if only there were branches to scrape against the house, or shutters to bang in the wind. . . . Oh well, the weather had come through beautifully for Halloween night, anyway.

Katie John stepped back into the kitchen to tend to the spaghetti, and immediately Heavenly Spot set up a howl, the likes of which only a Missouri hound dog can make: "O-o-o-o-O-O-O-o-o-o." Up and down the scale he told the world of his misery at being shut out on the back porch when a party was about to happen, with all its lovely dropped crumbs.

"Good, you sound fine," Katie said heartlessly. "That moaning makes wonderful Halloween sound effects."

Then she had one of those flashes of inspiration that made her wonder sometimes if she were a genius. Why not shut Spot up in a third-floor room to howl? (Mr. Watkins wasn't sleeping anyway.) When the girls listened through the speaking tubes, they'd hear this unearthly moaning!

She jerked the back door open again, and Heavenly Spot galloped in happily. His howling had never worked so fast before.

"Come on, Spot! Come on."

Katie John raced up the back stairs, Spot following eagerly, ears flapping, little knowing what new isolation he was about to suffer.

Only one third-floor room had a speaking-tube outlet. Katie John wedged open the speaking key so that Spot's howls would be sure to carry through the tubes, then shut Spot in the room.

"Okay, now howl all you want!"

Heavenly Spot obliged at full register on a scale that

rose as he heard his mistress' footsteps retreating down the stairs.

Now to find that bowl of spaghetti. This time she got it down to the basement without further incident. Setting the bowl in the coal cellar, she shut the door so it would be hidden. There now, every last thing was ready for the party. Ah! The doorbell was ringing. Katie ran up the basement stairs to answer it.

And then the party began. For there on the porch was Sue in her witch's costume, her plump face beaming under the pointed hat, looking about as scary as a loaf of homemade bread. Coming up the walk behind her were Priscilla Simmons and her two cronies. Priscilla was dainty as a Dresden-china shepherdess in laced bodice and full skirt. Betsy Ann wore a short Roaring Twenties dress with fringed skirt and dangling beads — really too old for her age, Katie John thought — and Carole Jo was a Gypsy. Katie was glad now she hadn't dressed as a fortuneteller, for Carole Jo's costume was more striking than the one Katie had planned first.

"Katie John! What are you?" the girls shrieked.

"She's the Black Ghost of Second Street Hill," said Sue, who'd been in on the secret of the costume, "and she's going to ha-aunt you!"

The black ghost whirled to set her rags in motion in the wind, stared hollowly out of her white eyes, and gave off gruesome chuckles. With wholehearted approval, the girls said she looked terrible.

Now more girls were arriving. Amidst their squeals and giggles over one another's costumes, Katie John set them to listening at the speaking tubes. She put her ear to the hole in the parlor first. Ah yes, Spot was doing a wonderful job. His far-off howling, filtered through the tubes, didn't sound like a dog at all, but simply a miserable, moaning something.

"Listen!" the black ghost said, opening wide her white eyes.

Priscilla put her ear up, and her face became startled. "Katie, what *is* that?"

"What is it? What is it?" The other girls crowded around to hear.

Katie led them to other speaking holes in the dining room and front bedroom, to take turns listening.

"It's my sister, the other black ghost," she said, trying not to laugh. "Who wants to go upstairs and call down to us through the tubes?"

The girls screamed and huddled together, but they were laughing too. Trust Katie John to fix up something weird for Halloween. At last Katie got some of them to follow her upstairs to talk through the tubes from empty bedrooms on the second floor. Miss Howell opened her door to call hello to the girls and watch the fun of witches, Gypsies, clowns, and tramps running about the halls.

In a back bedroom, Katie John was calling ghostly messages to the girls downstairs against the howling background when she noticed that the moan had softened to a throbbing note.

"Poor Spot, are you awfully miserable?" She reached down and patted his head, then realized — "Spot! What are you doing here?"

The brown dog's tail was a fast-wagging blur of happiness at his being loose.

"If you're here, then who's moaning? And how did you get out?"

For once she made good use of the speaking tube, calling to the girls downstairs, "Hey, is somebody down there moaning in the tubes?"

Three no's answered her. Quickly she rounded up the girls on the second floor and questioned them, but all denied moaning. She knocked on Miss Howell's door to ask, but Miss Howell only looked bewildered. The room where Spot had been! She ran up to the third floor, but the door to the room stood open and the room was empty. Surely somebody was playing tricks. Once before there had been strange noises in the tubes, but a perfectly natural explanation had turned up.

Running back down the stairs, she shouted, "Everybody come on!" and led the race down to the first floor. In the parlor she assembled all the girls, including the rest of the guests who'd arrived while she was upstairs. She counted. Thirteen girls, including herself. Everybody accounted for — nobody sneaking off to play tricks, Mother and Dad talking in the dining room. All right. Now. She put her ear to the speaking hole. The soft throb still sounded, rising, dropping, silent, then starting again.

"Look!" She cut through the girls' chatter. "Something different is happening. That first howling you heard was Spot, shut up in the third floor, but there's still moaning, and here he is!"

Heavenly Spot waved the white tip on his tail bliss-fully. Yes, here he was at last, in the midst of the party.

The girls broke out in an excitement of screams and talk.

"I don't like this!"

"I'm scared!"

"I want to go home!"

Then they all hushed to sudden silence as they heard another sound. Someone was coming down the stairs, slow, deliberate steps — thump, thump, thump — the feet of a Frankenstein monster. The thirteen girls were statues, holding their breath, watching through the parlor door to see what appeared at the foot of the stairs.

Mr. Watkins appeared. He was on his way to work.

Katie let out an involuntary giggle of relief, but the other girls still stood frightened at the sudden appear-ance of a big strange man.

"Good evening, Miss Katie," Mr. Watkins said. "I let your dog out. Shut up and crying, he was, upstairs."

"Oh —" No use trying to explain. "Thank you," said Katie. "Have a nice Halloween, Mr. Watkins."

"Thank you, miss," he said. "I don't think so."

The big man went out the front door, and the girls asked, "Who was *that?*"

"A renter," Katie John said briefly, putting her ear to the speaking-tube hole again. She'd hoped that somehow Mr. Watkins had been responsible for the moaning, but no — oh dear, there went the throb again — a sad sort of purr.

"It's still going," she whispered to the girls, most of

whom still looked frightened. "Dad, come here!" she appealed.

Dad came through the open folding doors from the dining room, and Katie asked him to listen at the hole.

"What *is* it?" She was half frightened now herself.

"It's a ghost," he said solemnly, "wailing in torment."

"Dad, stop it!" Katie cried. "This isn't funny."

He saw the horrified faces of the girls. "Spoil all my fun," he complained. "Oh, all right, you ninnies, it's the wind. The tubes moan like this when the wind is right."

"Oh, the wind!" The witches, Gypsies, tramps, and clowns laughed in relief and began chattering about how scared they'd been, and wasn't this fun. Katie John looked at her father doubtfully. She'd never noticed that effect in the tubes before, and she was unconvinced.

However, it was time now to get on with the party. Glancing at the clock on the mantel, Katie John saw that things were behind schedule.

"Fortunetelling time," she called gaily, leading the way to the dining room.

Witch Sue got the teams organized at passing apples under chins, while Black Ghost Katie sat down under the green chandelier to read Carole Jo's fortune. The fortunes were something of an anticlimax after all the excitement, but presently the party settled down to a comfortable buzz. Rhoda Phillips, in a voluminous clown costume, got the fortune about marrying a man from another planet, and was duly horrified and delighted. Priscilla, to Katie's disgust, drew the fortune predicting a present "smaller and better than you ever expected." She would. Katie half believed the fortunes herself by now; anyway it would be fun to see if any of them came true.

Katie John finished the fortunetelling before the apple race, interrupted whenever a girl dropped out for her fortune, was done. She was watching the laughing girls struggle with the apples when the doorbell rang. Being free, she went to answer it. Must be more trick-or-treaters.

"Trick or treat! Hey, is that you, Katie John?"

It was Howard Bunch, robed in a long shapeless dress and his mother's old hat. With him were Sammy and Pete, tramps, and a boy the size of sweaty Charles, wearing a gas mask. The girls' laughter came from the dining room, and Howard pushed forward.

"What's going on in there? Let's see."

Katie John understood. The boys intended to crash the party. Well, over her dead body! Let these boys in, and her whole party would disintegrate into a silly boy-and-girl thing. She just bet the girls would like it, too. Maybe Betsy Ann or Priscilla had even egged the boys to come.

"Oh no you don't!" She blocked him off with her arms. "Go on, you guys, we're busy!"

She slammed the door in their faces, and the doorbell promptly began to peal. Goodness, the girls would hear the commotion at the front. Let Betsy Ann know boys were out here, and she'd have them mixing in right away. She had to get the girls away before they found out.

Katie John ran to the dining room. "Quick! Come on! Downstairs! Quick!"

The girls ran after her, chattering and eager.

"Now what?"

"Where to?"

"What is it?"

Katie John herded them down the basement stairs, calling vaguely, "Something's about to happen!"

She pounded down the steps in the midst of the crowd, crying, "Hurry! Run — no, wait!" She'd remembered the tub of water and apples in the basement; someone might fall into it in the dark! She ran ahead and turned on the light. "Okay, come on! Watch out for the tub. Hurry!"

She raced the pack of girls into the fruit cellar and slammed the door on it, locking it. Now to get Dad. Have him get rid of those boys. Feet thudded outside, around the house. Oh no! The boys were running around looking for a way in. And there were windows in the fruit cellar on ground level. The boys would hear the girls — they'd see them in there. The girls would see the boys. Katie ran back, yanked open the fruit-cellar door, and the squealing girls poured out.

"It was dark in there!"

"Cold!"

"What's going on?"

"This way!" Katie John led the pack. Across the basement, around the corner, into the coal cellar; slam the door. Oh dear, no lock. Desperately she looked around while the girls shrieked in the dark. Ah, a chair. She wedged it under the doorknob.

"Wait!" she shouted.

Up the stairs she panted. "Dad, Dad!" Oh, where *was* he? There, coming in the front door.

"Dad, will you —"

"Just getting rid of some boys out there," he said at the same time.

"Oh, good," Katie gasped. She started away, running back down the hall to the basement steps.

She could hear the girls calling and pounding on the coal-cellar door. They were making plenty of noise, but they weren't laughing now.

"There." Katie gasped for breath, pulling away the chair and opening the door. "Wasn't — huff — wasn't that fun?"

"No!"

"I'm scared."

"I fell in the coal and got my costume dirty."

Tears watered in Rhoda's clown-painted eyes. "I want to go home." Her voice quavered.

Priscilla said quite calmly, "Katie John, did you know there was a bowl of spaghetti in there? I told the girls before somebody could think it was worms and be scared."

Well, that settled the spaghetti.

"Now then," Katie puffed, bright sparks before her eyes from all the running, "now then — oh yes — now for the apple bobbing."

She tried to get the girls organized at ducking for apples, but apples were a definite anticlimax after all the excitement and fright. Besides, Priscilla and some of the others didn't want to get their costumes wet.

"Well then, hide-and-seek," Katie John tried. "Let's play hide-and-seek down here with the lights out."

"No!" Rhoda wailed. "I'm scared down here."

"Me too!"

The whole party was falling apart. Rhoda was again starting to cry that she wanted to go home. But nobody ever went home from a party before refreshments. That was a time-honored rule.

Desperately cheerful, Katie John said, "Okay, time to eat, everybody! Let's go upstairs."

With relief and chatter and laughter now, the girls trooped up the steps after Katie John. Mother had all the food set out on the table, and the lighted pumpkin had a jolly gleam. Under the spell of bright lights and good food and lots of talk, the girls' nerves quieted down.

And by the time everything in sight was eaten and the guests started to leave, the girls were telling Katie John what a wonderful time they'd had.

"It was the best Halloween party I've ever been to!" they all seemed to agree.

When everyone had gone, Mother told Katie not to try to clean up the place; she'd do it. So Katie John went along to her room, so tired her feet seemed to be sinking down into her heels. She pulled off her costume, dropped it to the floor, and climbed into bed, too worn out even to wash the black off her face. As her body relaxed on the soft bed she gave a great sigh, but it was a sigh of satisfaction. Anyway, everyone had had a good time. So really, when you got right down to it, nothing had gone wrong!

The Eleven-year-old Blues

KATIE JOHN SAT CROSS-LEGGED on Sue's kitchen floor with Sue's kitten in her lap. The kitten, offspring of a neighbor's calico cat, was chubby, with black-and-white markings like a child's panda toy. He was struggling to get away to play, but Katie John held him up by his shoulders and looked into his face earnestly.

"Now then, Tibby, I'm going to put some kitty perfume on you to make you smell nice," she said. "You'll like it too."

From a box she took shredded catnip leaves and began rubbing them into Tibby's fur. The kitten twisted, sniffing at himself in surprise.

"Now go get Tiger," she told Sue, who was hovering by.

"Katie John, I just don't think it will work," Sue worried. "You don't know how Tiger hates Tibby. He really wants to kill Tibby. Just last night he drew blood —"

"That's exactly why we have to take the chance," Katie interrupted. "You can't go on shuffling cats back and forth forever."

"All right, but I don't think Janet is going to like it either," Sue said, going to the back porch where Tiger was shut up.

Tiger was Janet's cat, an arrogant old yellow tomcat who had ruled the Halsey household for lo, these many years. He'd reacted to the coming of Tibby with outrage, and his ruling passion was to dispose of this intruder. Mrs. Halsey (who was not at home) had said that it was too bad Tibby had turned out to be a boy; if he'd been a female cat, Tiger might have accepted him. As it was, the Halseys had to keep the cats apart, first putting one out, then another. After a week of "Don't let Tiger in! Tibby's in here!" Mrs. Halsey had proclaimed that if Tiger didn't get over his rage by Sunday, Sue would have to give Tibby back to the neighbor.

However, Katie John had come to the rescue. Her good idea was beautifully simple: Cats love catnip, so if Tibby smelled deliciously of catnip, Tiger would love Tibby. And ever after Tiger would love Tibby because he'd associate Tibby with something good.

She finished rubbing the leaves on the catnip-excited kitten and set him down on the floor. Immediately Tibby began to roll about, trying to get at himself, licking his fur in ecstasy. Good — then the leaves were fresh and potent, just as the pet-shop man had promised. Sue appeared at the door, awkwardly holding the big yellow cat, who was straining to leap from her arms.

"Is he ready?"

"Yes, hurry before the smell wears off."

148

Tiger dropped to the floor and crouched, ears back, as he saw the tumbling kitten. The yellow lines above his eyes were a scowl of hatred. A low, junglelike moan issued from his throat as he crept nearer to Tibby. Katie John drew in her breath. She'd never heard a cat make a sound like that. The girls grabbed up sofa pillows they had handy for throwing between the cats if a fight developed. Tiger inched toward the scrambling kitten, who was too absorbed in delight to notice approaching danger.

"Katie!" Sue whimpered.

The tomcat stopped, and his whiskers twitched. He sniffed in a puzzled way. Then he leapt forward! Sue screamed and held her pillow over her eyes, but Katie John laughed.

"Look!"

Tiger was leaning against Tibby, rubbing, smoothing, purring, eyes half closed in bliss. He adored this lovely catnip thing. He licked the black-and-white fur and sneezed. Oh joy, oh paradise! Lick, lick, lick, snuffle, toss it around, love it!

The girls shrieked with laughter as the old cat rolled onto his back, tossed the black scrap into the air, and caught it back with loving paws.

"He's got a catnip cat!" Katie John cried.

Tibby's little paws batted and played, and both cats licked, licked, licked the black fur in a frenzy of delight. Little murmurs of happiness came from the twisting mass of yellow and black and white cat fur. Sometimes Tibby licked himself, and sometimes his pink tongue licked yellow fur. The kitten's coat, however, was receiving the most licking. It was becoming slick and wet, wetter and wetter. Tibby began to look rather limp and tired. And presently he resembled a drowned cat, his fur as wet as if he'd been dipped in a bucket of water. But Tiger fairly bristled with excitement. Sue stopped laughing. The big tomcat was wearing out her kitten.

"Look at them play," Katie laughed. "Don't worry, from now on they'll be friends."

Tiger's batting paws were possessed with violence, and his fur stood on end. The pleasure sounds he was making became more like growls. On one throw the kitten landed heavily and gave a mew of protest.

And then with a moan Tiger sprang upon him and rolled over into a fighting ball, digging at the kitten with clawed hind legs, biting, snarling.

Sue screamed. She threw her pillow against the tomcat and snatched up the kitten, one hand marked with a scratch. Tiger stalked below, howling, lashing his tail, yellow eyes on the kitten.

"Oh heavens!" Katie John shooed her hands at the jungle beast, afraid he'd jump up at Sue. With the two pillows she managed to shove Tiger out to the back porch and shut the door.

Sue was examining the wet, exhausted kitten for bites or signs of blood, but the only wound seemed to be the beaded red line on her hand.

"They're not friends!" She turned furiously on Katie.

Katie John couldn't help laughing. "That's the understatement of the week!"

"Oh! Oh! How can you be so heartless!"

"Well — goodness — I'm sorry — I was —"

"Tibby almost got killed!" Sue was near to sobbing.

"I'm sorry. I just wanted to help. At first it —"

"That's right! It's all your fault! Honestly, Katie John Tucker, I'm never going to get mixed up in one of your good ideas again! And — and I wish you'd just go on home!"

"Fine!" Katie flared with responding anger. "I'll be so glad to!"

She slammed out the back door, aiming a kick at Tiger that missed. She'd only been trying to help. Well, it would be a long cold day before she'd ever help that ungrateful Sue Halsey again. How could Sue say that about her good ideas? Why, just last week she'd been glad enough to enjoy the Halloween party, one long evening of good ideas. It was so unfair. How was she to know Tiger would get so wild? He was nothing but a mean old vicious tomcat. Dangerous. They ought to get rid of him.

Still storming to herself, Katie John slammed into her own house, banging the glass-paned front door.

"Katie!" exclaimed Mother, who was coming from the front bedroom. "For heaven's sake, don't slam the door so. Do you want to break out all the panes?"

"That's right, yell at me!" Katie John yelled. "The minute I come in the house. Nobody cares if a person's best friend just — nobody cares if — you don't understand, and you don't want to!"

She ran down the center hall to the kitchen, where her father was having a cup of coffee, heading for her room.

"Ah, our little ray of sunshine," Dad began as his daughter whirled past.

"You don't understand either!" Katie shouted.

She slammed the door to her room, threw herself on her bed, and burst into tears.

First she cried about Sue and the cats, and about Mother and Dad never understanding. Then, as it often did when she cried, her misery widened to include everything else in the world that was wrong. Edwin a lost friend, acting so mean and disloyal, and the situation at school. That was the real trouble, she sobbed to herself. She still didn't know how to act with the girls. The Halloween party hadn't really helped after all. The girls were going right on leading their *little* life — chasing boys, getting worse if anything — and Katie still thought that was a disgusting way to grow up. Priscilla had come to school wearing a bra, though you couldn't notice until she mentioned it. And Betsy Ann and Carole Jo *sat* with some boys at the movies Friday night. Imagine how much fun *that* would be, with Howard throwing popcorn and all the catcalls and whistles of the boys up there in the balcony — so much noise you couldn't even hear the movie. She hated boys — she wouldn't want to be a boy! — and if the *little* life was how you had to act, she didn't know how to be a girl either. Everything she'd tried had failed.

Presently she heard her parents talking in low voices in the kitchen.

". . . why she's crying so much lately," Mother's voice murmured.

"She's got the eleven-year-old blues." Dad's next words were lost in his coffee cup, then, "— end of childhood. She's trying on roles. What to be: lady, clown, fairy princess —?"

"How do you know so much about eleven-year-old girls?"

How could Mother be so cruel as to laugh?

"Got one, haven't I, one of the best. . . . Mutter mutter . . . stormy time."

"Yes, I know. It's a stage. It will pass."

Katie John flung herself onto her back. She *hated* for her folks to talk about her as if she were somebody separate. "I'm not a stage," she thought, "I'm *me*." Dry-drained, she stared at the ceiling. She'd never felt so apart from her parents. If she didn't have this room by the kitchen, she wouldn't have to hear them talking about her. Tiny little cramped room. With all the rooms in this house, you'd think she could have a better one. If she had a room upstairs she could be off by herself.

Katie John wiped her wet cheeks and walked out to the kitchen. Keeping her voice very quiet, she said, "I would like to have a different bedroom."

Mother looked at her for a moment. "What did you have in mind, Katie John?"

"The upstairs back bedroom," she told them. It wasn't rented. She would like very much to live in Great-aunt Emily's old bedroom now.

"Very well," said Mother. "You may start moving your things right away."

Katie John didn't look at Dad, who thought he knew all about eleven-year-old girls.

Before supper was ready, Katie had all of her things moved up the back stairs to the back bedroom. After supper she would put everything away, fix things just as she wanted them. She laid a last stack of clothing on the bed and looked around the room. This was the room where she'd learned so much about Aunt Emily, whom she'd never seen, who'd died and left the house to the Tuckers. There was Aunt Emily's small rocker by the sewing table with the drawers; there was the old desk that had held Aunt Emily's letters. This was the room, too, that Gladys and Pearl, the western band-music lovers, had rented last winter — Katie John opened the French doors onto the balcony to let the feeling of them out. In the last dusk, made light by low white clouds, she looked down onto the vegetable garden, dried and blackened stalks now in early November, and the mulberry tree, nearly bare of leaves. The air from the open doors chilled Katie. Her very bones felt cold. "Now I'll be alone here," she thought.

In the morning when she awoke, it was as though only her eyes and the outside shell of her were alive. Inside her lone self she felt frozen to stillness, as if under her skin were frosty snow. Katie John's shell moved quietly through breakfast, waiting until the last minute to leave the house so that she might not have the misery of meeting Sue on the way to school, only to have Sue not speak to her. Even though she was late, her legs walked slowly on their lone way.

She arrived just as the last bell rang, and so missed the preschool passing around of the slam books. The slam books had been going around the day before, but Katie had been too absorbed in her catnip plans to pay attention to them. She became aware of them in the hall at recess when Betsy Ann handed her a black notebook.

"Here's my slam book," she said, giggling. "Write just whatever you want to."

At Kate's bewildered look, Betsy Ann explained. "Everybody" was making up slam books now. On each page was the name of someone in the class. Under each name you were to write exactly what you thought of that person, but not sign your name. Betsy Ann walked away so that she wouldn't see what Katie John wrote, while Katie examined the notebook. She recalled now that she'd seen black notebooks passed slyly from desk to desk yesterday.

Slam books were cruel and fascinating. Flattering to the popular, shattering to the not-so, they were deliciously anonymous, like the voice of Fate speaking. They were the sudden rage of the sixth grade.

Katie John read the first page, headed by Priscilla Simmons' name: "A darling girl." "Sweet." "Wish I was like her." "Roses are red, violets are blue. You are darling, wish I were you." "Pretty voice." And more and more until Katie could have thrown up. She flipped the pages to Sue's name. All nice things too, of course — in a way even better than Priscilla's page, for though everyone *admired* Priscilla, they *loved* Sue. The next page carried Rhoda's name, and now the stings, the "slams," appeared: "Too fat." "Hangs over people too much." "Ought to go on a diet." "Hate to be on a desert island with her — she'd eat everything in sight first." Katie winced for Rhoda's sake, even though she didn't really care much for the girl. She'd bet Howard wrote that.

There were boys' names in the book, of course. The boys had written extravagant insults to each other, and the girls had added a few, but it was also obvious that some of the girls thought the boys were pretty nice. Under Pete's name Katie found such remarks as, "Going to be an adorable tall basketball player." Someone had even found nice things to say about Howard.

Katie John saw her name on a page, but she flipped it over quickly, not looking at it yet for some reason. She carried the notebook back to her desk in the deserted schoolroom and sat down to study all the other pages first. The rating sheets for some of the names were hurtful in their bareness of remarks; some people weren't even interesting enough to inspire reactions. For one poor girl someone had written simply "Okay," and under it were a row of ditto marks, and not even many of those. On other pages the slams were violent: "I hate her." "Loud-mouth." "Sloppy." "Always picking his nose." "Why don't you wad yourself up in a ball and throw yourself away?"

Edwin's was one of the pages on which not much was written. Someone had written "Lone wolf," and there were a few ditto marks after that. However, someone else, obviously a girl, had written "I think he's cute." Katie's frozen snow stirred. And she muttered angrily to herself when she came to the comment, "Anybody who'd live in a graveyard is a weirdo."

"He can't help it if he has to live there," she said aloud. "Some people are so stupid!"

When she'd read every other page, it was time to turn to her own rating sheet. Her hand fumbled the leaves as she hunted it. There. Her eyes took in the page, and she saw that at least plenty of people had reactions to her. She'd received as many remarks as Priscilla and Sue. Her heart — not frozen after all? — pounded as she began to read:

"Sure knows how to give a party."

"A swell girl until she started acting so crazy."

"Crazy, man."

"Crazy in a nice way."

"Crazy-awful."

There were a few nice comments, such as "friendly" and "fun," but most of them were bad. "Hot-potato Katie is getting to be pretty sad apples." That would be Howard, Katie John thought angrily, remembering last winter when she'd carried hot potatoes in her pockets to keep her hands warm. And then there were, "Thinks she's so smart, but she's just a big wind." "Vulgar." "Hates boys." "Boy-hater." "Stuckup." "Don't like her." "Thinks she's too good for some people." And finally,

> "Some love big,
> Some love small,
> Katie doesn't love
> Anybody at all."

"And that's *right*," she thought viciously. Wait till she found a pencil! So that's what everybody thought of her. They hated her. Well, she'd just write down what she thought of them, too, every single last one of them. And glad of the chance!

Of course, some of the comments about her had been nice. And she'd be utterly fair. For a few people she had good things to say, but for the others — new snow fell inside of Katie John.

Starting at the front of the book, she wrote under Priscilla's name in an angry black scrawl, "So sickening sweet I could throw up." Howard: "Something that grew under a log." Sammy: "Obnoxious." Betsy Ann: "Great big nothing." She wrote that for several other girls with their lipsticks and their boy talk and their movie-star albums. Charles: "Stinks, and I really mean smells." At Sue's sheet she hesitated, then turned past it without writing anything at all. She paused over Edwin's page, too. None of the comments on her own page had seemed to come from Edwin. Still — her mind raced over all her troubles, and somehow she felt he'd started them all — still — Miserably she wrote, "The worst boy I ever knew." Then she threw the slam book down on Betsy Ann's desk and went to the girls' room, where she washed her hands until the bell rang for the end of recess. Too late she realized that the slam-book comments weren't so anonymous after all. Betsy Ann would read everything she'd written, and undoubtedly she'd tell. Katie should have passed the book on to other people first. Oh well! She didn't care!

Nobody liked her, so let them know she didn't like them either.

During class and the lunch hour Katie John watched the black notebooks surreptitiously being handed around. She noticed the unfriendly, suspicious, or even angry looks people were giving one another; especially she saw the black stares directed at her. Edwin didn't look at her at all. At noon Katie ate alone. In fact quite a few people were eating alone today, though Priscilla's gang huddled together, laughing and whispering over the books. A number of the girls had started books, so that one might presume there were duplicate comments in the notebooks. Even Howard and Sammy had slam books going around.

Katie John resisted the temptation to look at any more slam books, but the sight of them was as the constant poking of a sore tooth. At last, at afternoon recess, she took the notebook that a girl handed her. She didn't bother to read anyone else's rating sheet this time, but turned at once to her own. At first there were fairly light remarks, a sprinkling of good with the bad, reflecting yesterday's activity, but down the page the handwriting became black and violent — reactions to her slams in Betsy Ann's book. So what? She expected it, she firmly told the sting in her eyelids. And then she did give a little sob when she saw Sue's pretty, round handwriting: "A true and wonderful friend." Ah, Sue! And as a small warm spot in the snow began to melt, her eye automatically took in the neat printing below Sue's words: "What's become of Explorer Katie?"

Katie John looked at the words a long time. Not trying to figure out who had written them, for she knew. Only Edwin, and possibly Sue, would think of her as an explorer. No, she was trying to understand the meaning of the words. Did they mean he missed her company? That he wanted to make up? How could he have written that if he hated her so? The words didn't sound angry, though not warm either. Maybe he just put them down in his impersonal, studying-a-frog manner. And had he written them before or after he saw what she'd written about him in Betsy Ann's book? Maybe he hadn't seen it, or maybe he didn't know she'd written it. He'd know though, she was sure, the bottom of her stomach dropping away from the rest of her. She wondered if she wanted to change what she'd written about him. But then recess ended, and Mr. Boyle kept the class too busy for notebook passing for the rest of the afternoon. Edwin didn't turn around once to look at her, but Katie managed to catch Sue's eye across the room and gave her friend a big sunflower smile.

After school, the two friends were reunited. Katie John got her apology in first.

"Sue, I'm sorry," she exclaimed. "It really was all my fault. I should never have tried that with the catnip when there was a chance Tibby would get hurt."

"It's all right," Sue reassured her, eager to have all the badness over. "Tibby's all right. I shouldn't have gotten mad, even though I was worried."

The only blight on the girls' reunion was Sue's further news that Tiger still hated Tibby, and Tibby would have to go back to the neighbor. However, Mrs.

Halsey had suggested that Sue try to find a female kitten. Tiger obviously wouldn't stand for another male cat in the house to challenge his authority, but he might come to accept a female cat.

"I'll be on the lookout for a girl kitten," Katie John promised.

Something kept her from mentioning her new bedroom to Sue. It was a part of her new loneness, the trouble with her parents, and the *"little* life" of the girls, and nothing was settled there. There were still cold spots in Katie, and she became more conscious of them when she parted with Sue at the Halsey sidewalk.

When Katie John reached home, she walked right on up the front stairs, feeling like a renter, through the door to the back wing, down two steps, and around the corner to her bedroom. In the past, Katie's feelings had been clear, direct, violently happy or blackly miserable. But now what was this mixup of feeling about her new bedroom? It was good to go in and shut the door — a person with her own room, not just a cubbyhole off the kitchen in the midst of the family. She looked around the bedroom. It was big, space for all of her things; even had French doors on a balcony, something most girls didn't have. And yet — the room was part of the coldness, the loneness she'd chosen but wasn't sure she wanted.

For something to do she put away some more of her things and straightened drawers. In the move she'd unearthed quite a few things she'd forgotten she owned: a ukulele, a stamp book, some pictures, little ornaments. For a few minutes she planned how she might display these around the room, where she'd hang pictures and mementos. Then abruptly she shoved all the clutter into a corner and sat down in the rocker. Hands in her lap, she watched the light fade over the back yard.

After a time she became conscious of the sounds of supper preparations in the kitchen below her. She wandered down the back stairs and talked politely with Mother about what had happened at school today. There wasn't much to say because she didn't mention the slam books. Sue's cat trouble was a safer subject, and Mother said she would ask around for a female kitten for Sue. Mother and daughter found little else to discuss, so Katie John busied herself with setting the table.

A very quiet supper over, Katie John didn't know what to do with herself downstairs. She felt like a visitor with her parents. Homework. Yes, she should do her homework, for she certainly hadn't done much work at school today. Usually she studied at the dining-room table while her parents read and talked in the parlor. But now that needn't be. She had plenty of room for homework in her own bedroom. Katie John said a polite good night to her parents. Both smiled and kissed her good night as they always did, and she received the kisses, cold inside. She went back to her room.

Arranging her writing materials at Aunt Emily's desk, she tried to take some pleasure in the many slots and small drawers — a place for everything. But there was no pleasure in the world tonight. English assignment completed, she turned to her arithmetic drill in fractions. This was what she should have been doing late in the afternoon when she was watching Edwin across the aisle, wishing he'd turn around so she could see whether there would be friendliness in his face if she caught his eye. Could they be friends once more if she were the old Explorer Katie? But how could she ever be the old Katie again? So much had happened since last summer.

Katie John thought back, trying to figure out how things could have gone so wrong. Until the Street Fair she and Edwin had been friends, had had some wonderful times in their explorings. Then Priscilla Simmons had made her yell around about how she hated boys. Now how did that happen? Katie tried to remember the circumstances and who had said what, but it was too hard to sift out. It was the same with that horrible first day of school when Edwin had told her to stay away from him — she remembered that clearly enough, also her answer that she'd never speak to him again. But what had gone before? Katie shook her head over fractions that were a blur of squiggles. So much of it rested in the way people said things and the situation at the time.

If people had just left her and Edwin alone, they'd have gotten along all right. But you have to live with people. . . .

How did everything get so switched around? It used to be that the girls had ignored the boys, while she enjoyed roaring around with them. Last spring Priscilla and her friends had stood on the sidewalk talking, while Katie had played baseball with the boys on the playground. This fall she was the boy-hater, and though the girls were with her for a while, now they were edging up to the boys.

How had she ever gotten into this coil, as Cousin Ben called a mixed-up mess of trouble?

Katie John took off her clothes and lay down on her bed. Was that the perfectly normal way for a girl to grow up, doing all the silly little things the other girls were doing? Was she always going to be on the outside, the wrong foot, if she didn't follow along? What made her think she was so right and everybody else so wrong? She twisted onto her side, too miserable to cry. She hated herself for hating everybody. This was no way to live, torn up all the time, hating people, not knowing how to act.

She sat up in the dark, full of resolve. "Either I'll follow the crowd to womanhood," she thought dramatically, "or I'll just be me — whoever that is." Her thought ended on a weak note after all. She fell back on her pillow. For a moment she'd felt she was on the verge of solving things, but she just didn't know . . . she was so tired. She'd think about it in the morning.

In the night Katie John dreamed of walking a winding road. At last she came to a crossroads with a signpost, and she hurried forward to see which way to take. There were words on the arms of the signpost — words that would tell where each road led — but the words were blurred. Struggle though she did with her heavy eyelids, she couldn't get her eyes open wide enough to read the directions.

Netta's Picture Window

STRANGELY, she felt better when she awoke in the morning. Last night she hadn't settled a thing, yet somehow today she felt more comfortable in her mind. For a time she'd stay in this temporary cocoon with relief, not trying to probe at problems. It was a crisp November morning, the heaviness of clouds gone, sun shining on the last of brown leaves and bare branches. A good day for going nutting. The walnuts in the woods should be waiting in the nests of fallen leaves.

First, though, she should do something about yesterday's clutter of belongings pushed into a corner. She tried the ukulele on the top shelf of the desk and liked it there. With a small nail she hung Netta's fan over the bed. Head on side, considering how it looked, she thought of an old program of Great-aunt Emily's that she'd come across in moving her things. The program was of a chess-game pageant given at the church in 1897; Aunt Emily was the White Queen. With a thumbtack Katie put up the program under the fan. The program reminded her of a hand-painted and lacey doily that Aunt Emily had made, which Mother had given to Katie. On it was a drawing of a chubby child looking at a bird in a bush and saying, "Sing, Sweet Bird, and Cheer My Sorrow." Katie thumbtacked the doily next to the program. Well, might as well do this right. Working from the center fan out, she put up a snapshot of Sue, one of Heavenly Spot looking agreeable, Netta's picture, and some photos of old paddlewheel riverboats that she'd collected. There. She stepped back. Yes, it all looked fine — an interesting display over her bed.

She was still the visitor with her parents, however, as she went down the back stairs to breakfast — and she didn't run down the steps.

At the approach of Katie's quiet feet, Mrs. Tucker called out cheerfully, "Lots of work to do today."

Naturally. It was Saturday. Of course there'd be lots of work. Katie John sat down at the kitchen table, nodding politely to her father, who looked a little more awake than usual for eight o'clock in the morning.

The news was that the two rivermen, friends of last year's renter Mr. Peters, would be coming soon to put up for the winter. They'd be renting two third-floor rooms, and Mother wanted Katie to help her get them ready.

Carefully Katie John said, "And when I'm all done working, if there's any time left, may I go to the woods to get walnuts?"

"Why, certainly," said Mother, who was being as cheery as a jolly old Santa this morning. "When the work is done, you'll have the rest of the day for your fun."

" 'Dispose of your day as you think fit, but be here before eleven in the same disguise,'" put in Dad, trying a little humor. This was one of his favorite household quotes, from a story called "The Suicide Club" by Robert Louis Stevenson. Now that Dad was writing mystery books, he loved to quote from classic mysteries.

Katie John acknowledged her father's attempt with a small smile, but her thoughts were on the walnuts. At least they and the outing would be one good thing about today. The badness and problems of yesterday nudged, but she quickly blanked out that section of her mind. She wasn't ready to start turning over all that unhappiness again.

Mrs. Tucker set Katie to washing windows in the two third-floor rooms that the rivermen would rent. Katie John stood on a window seat to scrub one of the windows, looking through the leafless treetops to the river below. Lately the Mississippi had seemed to flow more slowly in its winter gray, but today the sun caught sparkles off the water, as if the river were saying, "I'm not ready to freeze over yet." On the opposite shore the sand at the water's edge was white, and the Illinois hills rose back from the river with still some brightness of autumn color brought out brave and cold in the sunlight.

It would be a nice view for a towboat man, Katie John thought. All winter he could watch his river. She imagined his practiced eye noting the breakup of ice in the spring, as he estimated to himself how long it would be before his boat would start running again.

For a moment she regretted her choice of a new bedroom. If she'd moved to the second-floor front bedroom, she could have had a view of the river too, instead of the balcony over the vegetable garden. But then she could always go outdoors to look at the river. That must have been what Netta had done at the farmhouse when she wanted to look at the view. Just the same, it was a shame her bridegroom hadn't planned the kitchen sink with a window looking out at the river. Had Netta been disappointed? Or had she helped plan the house? Maybe people didn't think much about views when they built houses in those days. Imagine not even having a window at all over your sink, where a woman spends so much time! Katie John was even more certain that she was right in her guess that Netta's clippings and pictures over her sink were her picture window.

The window washing didn't take too much of Katie's morning, for Dad had already washed the outsides. (Mother said it was too precarious a job for Katie to sit in the open windows working at the outside of the panes — all she needed was for Katie John to fall out of the third floor.) Next Katie threaded rods into the white curtains and hung them, and then she helped her mother make up the beds with clean sheets. At last she was free to go nutting.

She put a peanut-butter sandwich and an apple in a sack, found a burlap bag for the nuts, called Heavenly Spot, wheeled her bicycle out of the brick carriage house on the alley, and she was off for the day. Instead of "home free," as in hide-and-seek, she was "away free." Just for today no people or problems, just sun and woods and nuts.

Heavenly Spot was in a delight of galloping after the Explorer's wheels. As they neared the edge of town, Spot's nose whuffled eagerly at the autumn woods smells. Dutifully, however, the hound resisted side trails and stayed with his mistress until she dismounted her bicycle at Wildcat Glen. Then Heavenly Spot was free to follow his nose.

The walnuts were thick on the ground, just as she and Edwin had expected at the end of summer. How long ago that was — how could these even be the same nuts? Katie John began to scoop them into her burlap bag. "Now don't be greedy," she cautioned herself, "or the sack will be too heavy to carry home on the Explorer."

Presently the silence of the glen compelled her, and she stopped hurrying after nuts to sit on a stone in the sun and enjoy the peace of the spot. The creek flowed more busily over the rocks now than it had at the end of the summer. For a long time Katie John watched to see if the water ever made a different pattern of spray as it fell over a big rock. It never did. Without end the same slide, spurt, and sparkle of drops held true.

And all the time something else was going on in the back of her mind. She was waiting — waiting for something to develop. . . . And then the thought flowered full into the front of her mind. It was as if she'd known all along the main reason she'd come to Wildcat Glen today: she had to look at Netta's picture window again.

Leaving the sack of nuts by the creek, she got up,

climbed the rocky bank, and emerged from the trees into the field. Through the tall grass, white and dry with autumn, she walked to the weathered farmhouse.

In the kitchen she stood before the sink and looked up at Netta's picture window. Nothing had disturbed the scenes of California poppies, the pictures of different kinds of birds, the castle on the Rhine, and the river-raft scene in the middle of it all. Right in the middle — right in the center — something clicked into place. In matters of this sort you work from the center out. When she'd made the wall display over her bed this morning, she'd started in the middle with the fan, then worked out, thumbtacking up the other things in a widening circle. So here was the obvious clue to Netta's picture window. Work from the center out, and she'd know the order in which Netta had put up the clippings. Instead of a faded, tattered jumble on the wall, Netta's picture window would reveal a running diary of what she'd cared about the most. She'd learn Netta's story yet!

With excitement, Katie John began. Smack in the center, surely the first, was the picture of two boys on a raft floating down the river — a magazine drawing done in a bygone style. Still, it gave the feeling of lapping water and lazing on the sun-warmed boards of the raft, floating down and down the Mississippi.

"Oh yes," Katie John breathed softly. What difference if Netta had been a girl in the days of bustles and swoopy hats? She'd been a river kid, and she'd felt the call of the river the same as the boys. Maybe she'd even gone out on a raft once. And now that she was grown, a bride of, what — eighteen, twenty? — she'd put up the picture in memory of river-rafting days. Dear Netta. Katie hoped she'd gone rafting at least once before she had to put up her hair and be a lady.

Arranged around the river-raft drawing were the pictures of the castle, the shaggy camels, jagged snowy mountains. (The young bride had dreamed of faraway places, Katie interpreted to herself.) Also a couple of newspaper clippings. One was the poem about the delights of going barefoot. (If she'd gone river rafting and barefoot in those ladylike days, she must have been a tomboy.) The other clipping was a recipe for bleaching freckles. Across it, "Ha!" had been printed in heavy ink so many years ago. (Her freckles had bothered her, but she could laugh at herself when the recipe didn't work.)

Widening out in more or less of a circle, Katie John found next the articles on baby care, the page of pictures identifying different kinds of owls, and then the family things. There were the child's drawing of a house, the homemade valentine that said, "I love you, Mama," and Hal Calkins' signed drawing of an eagle. All these had been most important to Netta.

Katie John could see the farm wife coming through in the article of advice on when to plant vegetables according to the seasons and the time of the moon. But there were also clippings on how to trap animals of the woods without killing them, and how to make guest stations for wild animals. Had Netta done that with her children? Ah yes, remember the wildcat — had they shivered about the wildcat too?

Then came a faded newspaper clipping about the hard times farmers were having during the depression days, and how the President of the United States hoped to help them keep their farms. Next to it was a recipe for making your own soap, to save money. And finally, on the outside rim of the "picture window," colored magazine photos of California mountains and poppies, and the articles about business and farm opportunities in California.

So that's what had happened, why they'd left! Katie John had heard her parents speak of the depression years in the early 1930's, when so many people were poor, and farmers had lost their farms because they had borrowed money on their land and then couldn't pay back the money, or because they couldn't get good enough prices for their crops to make a living. Maybe that had happened to the Calkins family. California must have spelled a wonderful new chance. And Netta and her husband had been brave enough to take it. In July, 1932, the last month showing on the calendar by the stove, the Calkins family had moved out, gone to California.

There was an awful lot of guesswork in figuring out all that, Katie John realized. A real archaeologist probably would have needed lots more facts to go on. Some people might even say she'd just made it all up. But that was Netta's story as she understood it. She believed it.

And now that she knew Netta's story, what difference did it make? Why had she wanted so much to know about Netta? Why had she been drawn out here today, in the midst of all her troubles at school?

Katie John sat down in the left-behind rocker at the other end of the room. Something was about to happen, she felt, and she'd like to be sitting down for it. Each hand took hold of the other in her lap, and she sat without rocking.

It mattered because this tomboy Netta had managed to grow up to womanhood and still stay her own self. "Don't get mixed up in words," Katie John cautioned herself. Now, if ever, she must think straight. Netta hadn't been one of those sweet little girls who did nothing but play dolls and tea party. This girl with the honest freckled face (but don't forget the sparkle in her eyes that said, "I've a mind of my own") had her own special ways. *Just like me,* Katie thought. She'd had to come out of childhood into a terribly strait-laced, ladylike world. Yet she'd handled it all right and stayed herself.

The fan. Did it mean Netta had gone along with the crowd for a while, being a lady with her hair up? Katie John didn't believe that; else why had Netta kept the fan, treasured it? Maybe Netta had come to enjoy the womanliness that the fan stood for. Katie John wasn't sure what she herself meant by womanliness. She thought of the loveliness of a tall, slender figure, a lily swaying in a breeze. . . . Well, she'd find out about womanliness in time. Plenty of time. . . . And the reason why Netta had left the fan behind? Now the question didn't bother Katie. It might be simply that Netta had forgotten it. She'd been so busy getting her family ready for the move, so eager for the new life ahead. The important thing was that a tomboy girl had handled growing up.

"If she could do it, I can do it too."

Too excited to sit longer, Katie John ran out the back door into the sunlight. The November sun didn't carry much warmth, but inside of Katie was a glow that bathed her as the heat of summer. It was confidence in herself that had come flooding back. And not until it was there did she realize that she'd lost it in these past miserable months. Confidence in herself made all the difference in the world.

"Ah!" She breathed a great sigh of relief.

She became aware that she was standing in the weeds behind the farmhouse. It was as if she'd been away from the world and had finally come back to everyday things. What did she want out here? Her eye was caught by the gully where Edwin had been carrying on his "archaeological diggings." She hadn't even thought about his being around. Suppose he were?

Softly she approached the gully, but there were no sounds from it. A good deal of the trash had been cleared out of the ditch — the purse, the broken doll, the toy wagon wheels gone. She wondered what Edwin had done with all the leavings of the Calkins family. And then she saw that Edwin had dug a new ditch at right angles to the gully. It was a regular trench, going back across the gully's bank. Katie looked into it but saw nothing but dirt. Whatever was he digging for?

Edwin must be following some new idea here, some new adventure. All by himself. And she was left out.

Just think of all the fun they could be having on it together. If only they could make up. "How come you want to make up, if you hate him so?" Katie John demanded. "But I don't hate him," she answered herself honestly. "I miss him. I miss our good times together." All this time wasted in hating Edwin, going around hating the other boys at school. Edwin had made her mad, but she didn't really hate him.

It was even possible that part of their trouble was her own fault. She'd acted pretty mean herself, starting that war with the repulsives, not speaking to him, writing such a hateful thing about him in Betsy's slam book. Maybe she'd pushed him away just as much as he — Suddenly Katie John remembered the pitchfork, the unexplainable pitchfork in the Gypsy fortuneteller's cards. Had her own meanness to Edwin been like a pitchfork pushing him away?

"Oh, I don't hate him!" she said aloud.

As a matter of fact, she didn't hate the other boys either, not even Howard. Oh sure, Howard was sloppy and loud, obnoxious. But then who wasn't obnoxious sometimes?

"I sure was," Katie said aloud, shuddering, remembering the time she'd pretended to pick bugs off herself and eat them. What a nut she'd been. No wonder the kids had written what they had about her in the slam books, she'd been acting so crazy lately. Anyway, now she was at home with herself again. Maybe that was why she didn't hate boys any more. When you're at home with yourself, you don't have to go around hating people; you're at home with them too.

Katie John walked back past the farmhouse, stopping to look in the back door at Netta's clippings.

"Good-bye, Netta, old pal," she said. "Thanks!"

She ran across the field, slid down the creek bank, found her sack of nuts, and went to her bicycle. Heavenly Spot was lying beside it, panting after some lovely long chase. She'd forgotten to eat her lunch, so she ate the sandwich as she pedaled home. But the warm glow inside her didn't come from the food or the rays of the setting sun on her back.

When she reached home, the house was shadowy and quiet. Katie John put away her bicycle and left the walnuts in the basement. Coming upstairs, she wondered where her folks were. No one seemed to be around. She started on up the front stairs to her bedroom, and then she saw Mother sitting on the top step, her hands clasped around her knees.

"What's the matter? What are you doing?" Katie asked, coming up to her.

"Listening," Mother said, smiling. "I'm just listening to the house and its silence."

Katie John sat down on the step below her. So. So there was this to find out today too. Plain old practical Mother knew about listening to the house. Katie John digested this idea. For a time they sat together listening to the stillness. Something — a motor somewhere, perhaps the furnace or the refrigerator — made a rhythmic throb, as if the house were purring. Mother and daughter listened.

And when Mother asked where she'd been, Katie John thought that maybe her mother might understand after all. Just possibly. . . . Haltingly, Katie began to tell about Netta's picture window. It wasn't easy to put into words what she'd felt. In words, the whole thing didn't sound so dramatic and wonderful. As she finished, Mother murmured, "Yes, yes," nodding. But Katie John's new confidence wavered a little. It's all very well to think you can handle growing up. But what about school Monday?

"I still don't know just how I'm going to act with the kids at school," she admitted.

Mother reached around Katie's shoulders in one of her warm, old-time hugs. "Honey, you'll know when the time comes. Nobody knows just how he's going to act all the time. But we all have a sense of trueness that tells us what's right for us. In any situation, do what feels honest and right to you, Katie, and you won't go far wrong."

Katie John thought about it. Maybe Mother knew this, but she, Katie, didn't know this from experience yet.

At last she grinned. "Okay, I'll take your word for it. And every time I do something awful that you don't like, I'll just say it felt right for me to do it." She sprang up. "Now I've got an awful lot of nuts to crack."

Mother laughed and gave her daughter's bottom a light spank as Katie John ran back down the stairs.

Katie John and Edwin

MONDAY MORNING was the fourth morning that Katie John had awakened in her new bedroom. Each morning that she opened her eyes it was with a moment's surprise at finding herself in a strange bedroom. This time she hunched her pillow behind her and sat up against it, taking a good look at the room. Living in it no longer stood for being alone and hating her parents. Now that she was at ease with Mother and Dad again, should she move back to her old bedroom? Katie John relaxed against the pillow and decided, no. Sleeping in the cubbyhole of a room off the kitchen was being a child in a nursery in the heart of the family. It was time for her to be more on her own now. She didn't want to go back to being "little" Katie John.

She jumped out of bed and took a certain care in dressing for school. She had a feeling she'd be better able to handle things if she were well put together. First there was the problem of the slam books and the hateful things she'd written in them. When she'd left school Friday, everybody had been mad at her. And now she didn't even mean most of the things she'd written. The first thing she had to do was get hold of those slam books and change what she'd written. For Howard she'd change, "Something that grew under a log" to — let's see, what was Howard? — "The wild man of sixth grade!" Katie chuckled.

And what would she write for Edwin? She certainly didn't really believe he was "the worst boy" she ever knew. Katie John moved on to the bigger and most important problem: how was she going to make up with Edwin? Because that was what she really wanted. It wasn't going to be easy. She couldn't simply walk up to him and say "I'm sorry." You had to say what you were sorry for. Sorry that things had gotten all mixed up, sorry that she'd been floundering around in six different directions the last couple of months, sorry that they weren't friends any more? She couldn't say any of that. She'd feel dumb. And Edwin would feel dumb too. Besides, there was her boy-hater reputation to complicate matters. What would Edwin think if she just started talking to him again, hanging around him? What would the other kids think?

Katie John set off for school feeling as if she were walking a tightrope — anxious, not knowing what the day would bring, having to be careful of the steps she took at school today.

Walking with Sue, she confessed, "I wrote a lot of horrible things about people in those slam books."

"I know," Sue said.

"I'm going to change what I wrote. I guess I didn't really mean those things."

"I know, Katie," said her true and loyal friend.

They arrived at school in plenty of time before the

first bell. Sue had to go in to set up equipment for a weather project. Katie went looking for the girls and their slam books. On the playground Howard and some of the boys were measuring off chalk lines to mark the downs for a football game, stretching across brown twine from a large ball as a guide for the chalk. She didn't see Edwin with them — oh, there he was, leaning against the school wall whittling at a piece of wood with his knife. And there were Priscilla and Betsy Ann on the sidewalk looking at black notebooks. Trying to seem casual, Katie sauntered over to the girls.

"Uh — mind if I see your slam book?" she asked Betsy Ann.

Betsy Ann looked at her rather coldly. "This isn't a slam book," she said. "It's my movie-star album."

"We aren't doing slam books any more." Priscilla shrugged as if they were a matter of the distant past.

"Why? Don't you think you wrote enough, Katie John?" Betsy Ann said.

"Well — not that — I just wanted to change a few things," Katie John said humbly.

"Our mothers called each other up over the weekend and said the slam books weren't very nice, and we had to stop," Priscilla explained, unfreezing a little.

"I guess we'd all like to change a few things." Betsy Ann giggled forgivingly.

Katie John was grateful for that giggle. Nevertheless, she was frustrated. Too late. Her black scrawls would have to stand in the other kids' minds.

The girls went on with their photo-album business.

"I'll trade you two Pretty-Boy Hughes for one Ricky Arno," Betsy Ann bargained.

"Oh sugar, I don't know." Priscilla hesitated. "I've only got two Rickys, and he's so darling. Maybe if you'd give me a Bonnie Jones too. . . ."

Katie John's distaste ruffled. Honestly! She opened her mouth to say something scornful, and then she closed it again. If she wanted the right to follow her own special ways, then the girls had that right too. If they wanted to waste time on photo albums, that was their business, not hers to fuss about. Actually, when you got right down to it, they hadn't tried to force her to have albums. Nobody had said, "Katie John, if you don't have an album, we won't like you."

Let them have their boring books. Uninterested, she wandered away, and then stood uncertainly. There was another twenty-five minutes before class took up. What *did* she want to do? Well, she knew what she'd *like* to do; she'd like simply to walk up to Edwin and ask him what he was digging for now out at Wildcat Glen. Just then Edwin looked up. His glance met hers and moved away without a sign of recognition. Katie's chest seemed to tighten narrower. How was she ever going to make up with Edwin?

As she stared toward the playground, gradually she became aware of the boys playing football. It wasn't a real game, for there weren't enough boys for even sides. And they weren't allowed to play tackle, only tag football. But they were having fun, and there was so much scuffling that already you could hardly see the chalk lines they'd measured so carefully with the twine.

The air was crisp; a little breeze stirred Katie's hair in the sunshine. It was a perfect morning for football. Last fall she and a couple of the other girls had played football with the boys every morning before school. She'd developed a pretty catchy weave at running with the ball, though she'd never been any good at kicking. Huh, she could run the ball a lot better than that old Howard. She wished she were out there, twisting and running and laughing. Next year in junior high there wouldn't be any chance to play football with the boys at all, for the boys and girls divided into separate gym classes, and they'd all be so much older. This fall was probably her last chance. To be perfectly honest with herself, that's what she wanted to do: roar around with the ball and the boys. Without thinking further, Katie John ran into the skirmish.

"Hey, Sammy," she shouted, "pass it here!"

Caught up in the excitement of the game, Sammy handed off the ball to Katie, and she ran it down the field, twisting and darting. Finally long-legged Pete tagged her. The game went on. After the next kick, Katie John pounded down the field with the boys, yelling happily. Then the other side went into a brief huddle. Waiting, Katie John's eye lit on the rolled-up ball of brown twine lying at the side, and a wonderfully wicked idea sparked. That ought to spice up the game even more! No one was watching as Katie John slipped the ball of twine under her jacket.

The boys came out of the huddle, yelling encouragement to each other, and the game continued. Another kick, and Howard, next to Katie, caught the ball. She raced along beside him and managed to trip him so the football flipped out of his hands. Quickly she passed the ball of twine to Sammy, who was on her side.

"Here you go, Sammy!"

Sammy darted away in the other direction with the ball of twine, while Howard, Pete, and the others roared after him, shouting, "He's got it! He's got it!"

"Down here! Down here!" urged sweaty Charles, near the goal line.

Sammy made a long pass to Charles, and the ball flew through the air, unwinding a ribbon of twine.

"Hey, the ball's coming apart!" somebody yelled, but Charles was only concentrating on catching the ball. He received it and ran toward the goal line. Howard grabbed the end of the twine and ran in the opposite direction.

"Hey, what a crazy ball!" Whooping, the other boys snatched at the unraveling string between Howard and Charles and tangled in it.

"Hey, you guys, touchdown!" Charles yelled, standing over the goal line. Then he looked stupidly at the end of the twine he was holding.

Katie John doubled up, shrieking with laughter. "Yeah, touchdown!" she echoed, gasping between rolls of "Ha ha ha!"

The girls on the sidelines were screaming with laughter too at the crazy, mixed-up football game — especially at the tangle of boys and twine between Charles and Howard, each staring in amazement at his end of the string.

"Does this touchdown count?" Charles said doubtfully. And everyone went into gales of laughter again.

Katie John saw that Edwin on the sidelines was laughing too. Say, that's right, he hadn't been in the game. As a matter of fact, Edwin was often doing something alone when the other boys were playing.

Oh, he messed around with them sometimes, but he was pretty much of a lone wolf. Suddenly Katie John thought of something: If Edwin's best friend was a girl who hated boys, what did that make Edwin? A sissy? Was it something like that that had made the trouble? Of course Edwin was no sissy, but had he thought it would look that way?

But then, here she was playing football with the boys. It should be obvious now to the kids that she didn't hate boys. So . . .

"I did it! I simply did what I felt honestly right at the time—playing football with the boys."

And now as a result, maybe — Katie John grinned wholeheartedly at Edwin. And Edwin, still laughing, grinned back.

In fact, everyone was still laughing at the efforts of the boys to unsnarl themselves from the twine.

"Trust Katie John to do something like this," somebody said.

"Yeah," said Howard half in disgust, half in admiration. "Only a girl would think of a thing like this, queering up good plain old football."

"So what, I *am* a girl!" said Katie John.

She pulled her skirt around into place and smoothed down her spiked-out bangs. Then her hand went on to fluff out the waves of her hair in a feminine gesture that came quite naturally.

As she walked over to Edwin, she heard some boy say, "Katie John sure is a nutty girl."

And Betsy Ann replied, "Yes, she's all right."

Katie John walked up to Edwin. And then she didn't know what to say.

"That was fun," she said, trying to carry along on the strength of the game's excitement.

But Edwin wasn't laughing now. He looked as awkward as Katie John was beginning to feel. For a minute she thought he wasn't going to speak.

Then he said, "I thought you hated boys."

"Well, I don't," she said firmly. "I guess — boys are just people."

"Huh." He poked his toe at a pebble, watching it carefully as if the pebble might get away. "Huh — I thought you weren't ever going to speak to me again."

"Well — I'm sorry that I — that is — Now look, Edwin Jones, I'm trying to be friends, so you just quit being so hard to get along with!"

Katie John watched him anxiously.

Finally Edwin looked up and grinned. "Okay, Katie John."

Abruptly he stuck out a dirty hand. Katie John looked at it, then understood. She put out her own hand, and they shook on it.

To get over the embarrassment of the moment, Katie plunged into talking.

"I saw that trench you dug out at the deserted farm. What are you digging for?"

"Indian stuff!" Edwin's face lit up even more. "Katie John, I think I've found an old Indian burial mound!"

Eagerly he told how he'd come across a stone hatchet in the gully bank while he was digging back for more of the Calkins' things. Now he was digging the trench, carefully picking away at the earth so as to find things just as they lay, the way archaeologists dig. Already he'd found an earthen pot with only a few pieces broken off. But he hadn't come to any bones yet.

"Buried treasure!" Katie John exclaimed, suddenly remembering the Gypsy fortuneteller at the Street Fair. Another prediction had come true!

But Edwin knew nothing of the fortuneteller, and he hurried on as if he'd been storing up words for two months.

"It could be the burial mound of some of the Sac and Fox Indians. I've been reading up on them, and they were the tribes that lived around here mostly. When I've got more to go on, I'm going to tell Mr. Boyle, and maybe he'll notify the archaeology professor at the state university. But first I've got to dig some more to be sure."

"I could help!"

"Yeah, I could use you. We've got to hurry before the ground gets too frozen this winter to dig. Just think, Katie John, maybe next spring the man from the university might bring his students over here. We could watch a real dig!"

"Yes!" But Katie's sigh was really a great big breath of relief. Things were going to be all right between her and Edwin.

Just then a familiar chant sounded. It was Howard.

"Katie's got a boy friend! Katie's got a boy friend!"

Casually Edwin shouted back, "Aw, go climb a tree."

"Go chase yourself!" Katie John called out at the same moment.

They looked at each other in surprise at expressing the same idea at once. And then the two friends began to laugh together as the school bell rang.